Also in Fontana

The Fontana Book of Great Horror Stories
The 3rd Fontana Book of Great Horror Stories
The 4th Fontana Book of Great Horror Stories
Ed. Christine Bernard
The 5th Fontana Book of Great Horror Stories
The 6th Fontana Book of Great Horror Stories
The 8th Fontana Book of Great Horror Stories
Ed. Mary Danby

The 2nd Fontana Book of Great Ghost Stories
The 4th Fontana Book of Great Ghost Stories
The 6th Fontana Book of Great Ghost Stories
The 8th Fontana Book of Great Ghost Stories
Ed. Robert Aickman
The 9th Fontana Book of Great Ghost Stories
Ed. R. Chetwynd-Hayes

London Tales of Terror
Ed. Jacquelyn Visick
Scottish Tales of Terror
Ed. Angus Campbell

The Elemental
R. Chetwynd-Hayes
Lord Halifax's Ghost Book
Lord Halifax
The Valley of Spiders
H. G. Wells

CORNISH
Tales of Terror

Edited by R. Chetwynd-Hayes

Collins
FONTANA BOOKS

First published by Fontana Books 1970
Second Impression February 1971
Third Impression June 1974

Made and printed in Great Britain by
William Collins Sons & Co Ltd Glasgow

CONTENTS

ACKNOWLEDGEMENTS

The Editor gratefully acknowledges permission to reprint copyright material to the following:

Miss Daphne du Maurier and Messrs Curtis Brown Ltd for THE BIRDS.

Messrs J. M. Dent & Sons Ltd for ROLL-CALL OF THE REEF by Sir Arthur Quiller-Couch from WANDERING HEATH.

The Royal Literary Fund for THE IRON PINEAPPLE by Eden Phillpotts from PEACOCK HOUSE.

Messrs MacMillan & Co Ltd for ALL SOUL'S NIGHT by A. L. Rowse from CORNISH TALES.

R. Ellis Roberts and Cecil Palmer for THE NARROW WAY, from THE OTHER END.

The Estate of J. D. Beresford and Sidgwick & Jackson Ltd for THE MISANTHROPE from NINETEEN IMPRESSIONS by J. D. Beresford.

Sir Rupert Hart-Davis for MRS. LUNT by Sir Hugh Walpole.

Except where otherwise stated, the short items between the stories have all been taken from 'Popular Romances of the West of England' by Robert Hunt, 1871.

EDITOR'S NOTE

Every effort has been made to trace the owners of the copyright material in this book. It is the editor's belief that the necessary permissions from publishers, authors and authorised agents have been obtained but in the case of any question arising as to the use of any material, the editor, while expressing regret for any errors, will be pleased to make the necessary correction in future editions of the book.

INTRODUCTION

It may truthfully be said, 'One man's terror is another man's fun.'

Count Dracula may appeal to one reader's humour, Frankenstein's monster to his pity, but many have shuddered when confronted by these fictional horrors. I do not propose to write an essay on what inspires pleasurable terror, for the very good reason that I do not know. I can only judge by my own taste and, as I have illustrated, this may not be shared by anyone else. So for that reason, among others, I have tried to make this collection as varied as possible.

Cornwall is the ideal setting for a tale of terror. Wreckers luring ships on to rocks, Piskies that gallop a farmer's horse half to death on a moonlit night, Giants who hurl great boulders at each other, Mermaids who: 'Comb their hair, yellow as gold, by the noontide sun, at the water's edge', the fairy miners known as 'Knockers', phantom ships that sail over the moors—Cornwall has them all.

Sir Arthur Quiller-Couch has dealt with the wrecker theme in his ROLL-CALL OF THE REEF. It needs little imagination to make one's hackles rise when reading:

'And while the drum beat, and my father held his breath, there came up out of the sea and the darkness a troop of many men, horse and foot, and formed among the graves; and others rose out of the graves and formed up—drowned Marines with bleached faces, and pale Hussars riding their horses, all lean and shadowy . . .'

There is a thoughtful little story called THE MISANTHROPE, by J. D. Beresford, about a man living alone on an island just off Trevone. What is it that makes him so reluctant to look back over his shoulder? Then there is the famous story, THE BOTATHEN GHOST, by R. S. Hawker, sometime Vicar of Morwenstow, which has the virtue (or so it is reputed) of being true. I have included ALL SOULS' NIGHT, by A. L. Rowse, partly because of its genuine Cornish background, but mainly for its leisurely style. This is the way a ghost story should be told: quietly, with the old dean smoking his cigar, and breaking off now and again to send a junior fellow for a whisky and soda. Again there is the question: what is horror? I find old Lady Lantyan, who fed her chaplains on rice, currants and old brandy, at least as terrifying as the ghost that pops up at the end.

THE NARROW WAY, by R. Ellis Roberts, is a Cornish Tale of Terror with a difference: a black miracle. The reader may be inclined to wonder just how much of this story is true, and possibly come to the conclusion that somewhere in Cornwall's long, chequered history there once lived a clergyman like the mysterious Frank Lascelles.

A word about THE PHANTOM HARE. I found this in a bound edition of Argosy Magazine dated January-June 1879. The only clue to authorship are the initials M. H., and Fleetway House have been unable to help me on this point. Back in 1879, Argosy was edited by Mrs Henry Wood of *East Lynne* fame. I was pleased to find this story because the Cornish legend of the white hare is an intriguing one. Robert Hunt in his POPULAR ROMANCES OF THE WEST OF ENGLAND writes:

'It is a very popular fancy that when a maiden, who has loved not wisely but too well, dies forsaken and broken hearted, she comes back to haunt her deceiver in the shape of a white hare. This phantom follows the false one everywhere, mostly invisible to all but him. It sometimes saves him from danger, but invariably the white hare causes the death of the betrayer in the end.'

THE IRON PINEAPPLE, by Eden Phillpotts, is a subtle piece of macabre, told with a certain amount of underlying humour, but at the same time portraying the horror of a mind possessed by an obsession. WISH ME LUCK, by H. A. Manhood, is a breath of old Cornwall, with a little twitch of terror that comes when you least expect it.

Having, so to speak, cut my literary teeth on Hugh Walpole's *Rogue Herries* novels, it gave me much personal satisfaction to be able to include MRS LUNT in this collection. Walpole was undoubtedly at his best when writing a Cornish ghost story. How about this to send the cold shivers running up your spine?

'My heart bounded. There, standing just in front of the trees, as though she were waiting for us, was the old woman whom I had seen in my room the night before. I stopped. "Why, there she is!" I said. "That's the old woman of whom

I was speaking—the old woman who came to my room." He caught my shoulder with his hand. "There's nothing there," he said. "Don't you see that that's shadow? What's the matter with you? Can't you see that there's nothing?" '

Robert Hunt's THE SPECTRE BRIDEGROOM is a fireside ghost story. There is no attempt at dialogue, the tale is related just as many a Cornish housewife must have told it down through the years. This is pure Gothic horror.

No anthology of Cornish Terror Tales would be complete without Daphne du Maurier's THE BIRDS. You may have seen the excellent film made by Alfred Hitchcock, but I still urge you to read the story. The horror comes with deceptive quietness, from the calm of a peaceful Cornish background. For example:

'Nat woke just after two and heard the east wind, cold and dry. It sounded hollow in the chimney, and a loose slate rattled on the roof . . . He drew the blanket round him, leaned closer to the back of his wife, deep in sleep. Then he heard the tapping on the window-pane. It continued until, irritated by the sound, Nat got out of bed and went to the window. He opened it; and as he did so something brushed his hand, jabbing at his knuckles, grazing the skin. Then he saw the flutter of wings . . .'

I have closed the collection with a story of my own, THE BODMIN TERROR. This is the result of taking people I know, casting them in bizarre roles, then allowing imagination to do the rest. I hope you like the finished product.

Finally, between the stories are short items concerning specific locations in Cornwall. These are mainly Cornish Folk stories and may well be of interest if you are thinking of visiting the county. I can only hope they do not frighten you away and thereby ruin the Cornish tourist trade.

R. CHETWYND-HAYES

THE LIMP CORPSE

An Old Cornish Superstition

If a corpse stiffen shortly after death, all is thought to proceed naturally; but if the limbs remain flexible, someone of the family is shortly to follow. If the eyes of a corpse are difficult to close, it is said 'they are looking after a follower'.

ROBERT HUNT

THE ROLL-CALL OF THE REEF

SIR ARTHUR QUILLER-COUCH

'Yes, sir,' said my host the quarryman, reaching down the relics from their hook in the wall over the chimney-piece; 'they've hung there all my time, and most of my father's. The women won't touch 'em; they're afraid of the story. So here they'll dangle, and gather dust and smoke, till another tenant comes and tosses 'em out o' doors for rubbish. Whew! 'tis coarse weather.'

He went to the door, opened it, and stood studying the gale that beat upon his cottage-front, straight from the Manacle Reef. The rain drove past him into the kitchen, aslant like threads of gold silk in the shine of the wreckwood fire. Meanwhile by the same firelight I examined the relics on my knee. The metal of each was tarnished out of knowledge. But the trumpet was evidently an old cavalry trumpet, and the threads of its parti-coloured sling, though frayed and dusty, still hung together. Around the side-drum, beneath its cracked brown varnish, I could hardly trace a royal coat-of-arms, and a legend running—*Per Mare per Terram*—the motto of the Marines. Its parchment, though coloured and scented with wood-smoke, was limp and mildewed; and I began to tighten up the straps—under which the drumsticks had been loosely thrust—with the idle purpose of trying if some music might be got out of the old drum yet.

But as I turned it on my knee, I found the drum attached to the trumpet-sling by a curious barrel-shaped padlock, and paused to examine this. The body of the lock was composed of half a dozen brass rings, set accurately edge to edge; and, rubbing the brass with my thumb, I saw that each of the six had a series of letters engraved around it.

I knew the trick of it, I thought. Here was one of those word padlocks, once so common; only to be opened by getting the rings to spell a certain word, which the dealer confides to you.

My host shut and barred the door, and came back to the hearth. ''Twas just such a wind—east by south—that brought in what you've got between your hands. Back in the year 'nine it was; my father has told me the tale a score o' times. You're twisting round the rings, I see. But you'll never guess the word. Parson Kendall, he made the word, and locked down a couple o' ghosts in their graves with it; and when his time came, he went to his own grave and took the word with him.'

'Whose ghosts, Matthew?'

'You want the story, I see, sir. My father could tell it better than I can. He was a young man in the year 'nine, unmarried at the time, and living in this very cottage just as I be. That's how he came to get mixed up with the tale.'

He took a chair, lit a short pipe, and unfolded the story in a low musing voice, with his eyes fixed on the dancing violet flames.

'Yes, he'd ha' been about thirty year old in January, of the year 'nine. The storm got up in the night o' the twenty-first o' that month. My father was dressed and out long before daylight; he never was one to 'bide in bed, let be that the gale by this time was pretty near lifting the thatch over his head. Besides which, he'd fenced a small 'taty-patch that winter, down by Lowland Point, and he wanted to see if it stood the night's work. He took the path across Gunner's Meadow—where they buried most of the bodies afterwards. The wind was right in his teeth at the time, and once on the way (he's told me this often) a great strip of oar-weed came flying through the darkness and fetched him a slap on the cheek like a cold hand. But he made shift pretty well till he got to Lowland, and then had to drop upon his hands and knees and crawl, digging his fingers every now and then into the shingle to hold on, for he declared to me that the stones, some of them as big as a man's head, kept rolling and driving past till it seemed the whole foreshore was moving westward under him. The fence was gone, of course; not a stick left to show where it stood; so that, when first he came to the place, he thought he must have missed his bearings. My father, sir, was a very religious man; and if he reckoned the end of the world was at hand—there in the great wind and night, among the moving stones—you may believe he was certain of it when he heard a gun fired, and, with the same, saw a flame shoot up out of the darkness to windward, making a sudden fierce light in all the place about. All he could find to think or say was, "The Second Coming—The Second Coming! The Bridegroom cometh, and the wicked He will toss like a ball into a large country!" and being already upon his knees, he just bowed his head and 'bided, saying this over and over.

'But by'n'by, between two squalls, he made bold to lift his head and look, and then by the light—a bluish colour 'twas—he saw all the coast clear away to Manacle Point, and off the Manacles, in the thick of the weather, a sloop-of-war with top-gallants housed, driving stern foremost towards the reef. It was she, of course, that was burning the flare. My father could see the white streak and the ports of her quite plain as she rose to it, a little outside the breakers, and he guessed easy enough that her captain had just managed to wear ship, and was trying to force her nose to the sea with the help of her small bower anchor and the scrap or two of canvas that hadn't yet been blown out of her. But while he looked, she fell off, giving her broadside to it foot by foot, and drifting back on the breakers around Carn dû and the Varses. The rocks lie so thick thereabouts, that 'twas a toss up which she struck first; at any rate, my father couldn't tell at the time, for just then the flare died down and went out.

'Well, sir, he turned then in the dark and started back for Coverack to cry the dismal tidings—though well knowing ship and crew to be past any hope; and as he turned, the wind lifted him and tossed him forward "like a ball," as he'd been saying, and homeward along the foreshore. As you know, 'tis ugly work, even by daylight, picking your way among the stones there, and my father was prettily knocked about at first in the dark. But by this 'twas nearer seven than six o'clock, and the day spreading. By the time he reached North Corner, a man could see to read print; hows'ever, he looked neither out to sea nor towards Coverack, but headed straight for the first cottage—the same that stands above North Corner to-day. A man named Billy Ede lived there then, and when my father burst into the kitchen bawling, "Wreck! wreck!" he saw Billy Ede's wife, Ann, standing there in her clogs, with a shawl over her head, and her clothes wringing wet.

' "Save the chap!" says Billy Ede's wife, Ann. "What d' 'ee mean by crying stale fish at that rate?"

' "But 'tis a wreck, I tell 'ee. I've a-zeed'n!"

' "Why, so 'tis," says she, "and I've a-zeed'n too; and so has everyone with an eye in his head."

'And with that she pointed straight over my father's shoulder, and he turned; and there close under Dolor Point, at the end of Coverack town, he saw another wreck washing, and the point black with people, like emmets, running to and fro in the morning light. While he stood staring at her, he heard a trumpet sounded on board, the notes coming in little jerks, like a bird rising against the wind; but faintly, of course, because of the distance and the gale blowing—though this had dropped a little.

'"She's a transport," said Billy Ede's wife, Ann, "and full of horse soldiers, fine long men. When she struck they must ha' pitched the hosses over first to lighten the ship, for a score of dead hosses had washed in afore I left, half an hour back. An' three or four soldiers, too—fine long corpses in white breeches and jackets of blue and gold. I held the lantern to one. Such a straight young man."

'My father asked her about the trumpeting.

'"That's the queerest bit of all. She was burnin' a light when me an' my man joined the crowd down there. All her masts had gone; whether they carried away, or were cut away to ease her, I don't rightly know. Anyway, there she lay 'pon the rocks with her decks bare. Her keelson was broke under her and her bottom sagged and stove, and she had just settled down like a sitting hen—just the leastest list to starboard; but a man could stand there easy. They had rigged up ropes across her, from bulwark to bulwark, an' beside these the men were mustered, holding on like grim death whenever the sea made a clean breach over them, an' standing up like heroes as soon as it passed. The captain an' the officers were clinging to the rail of the quarter-deck, all in their golden uniforms, waiting for the end as if 'twas King George they expected. There was no way to help, for she lay right beyond cast of line, though our folk tried it fifty times. And beside them clung a trumpeter, a whacking big man, an' between the heavy seas he would lift his trumpet with one hand, and blow a call; and every time he blew, the men gave a cheer. There (she says)—hark'ee now—there he goes agen! But you won't hear no cheering any more, for few are left to cheer, and their voices weak. Bitter cold the wind is, and I reckon it numbs their grip o' the ropes, for they were dropping off fast with every sea when my man sent me home to get his breakfast. Another wreck, you say? Well, there's no hope for the tender dears, if 'tis the Manacles. You'd better run down and help yonder; though 'tis little help that any man can give. Not one came in alive while I was there. The tide's flowing, an' she won't hold together another hour, they say."

'Well, sure enough, the end was coming fast when my father got down to the point. Six men had been cast up alive, or just breathing—a seaman and five troopers. The seaman was the only one that had breath to speak; and while they were carrying him into the town, the word went round that the ship's name was the *Despatch*, transport, homeward bound from Corunna, with a detachment of the 7th Hussars, that had been fighting out there with Sir John Moore. The seas had rolled her further over by this time, and given her decks a pretty sharp list; but a dozen men still held on, seven by the ropes near the ship's waist, a couple near the break of the poop, and three on the quarter-deck. Of these three my father made out one to be the skipper; close by him clung an officer in full regimentals—his name, they heard after, was Captain Duncanfield; and last came the tall trumpeter; and if you'll believe me, the fellow was making shift there, at the very last, to blow "*God save the King*." What's more, he got to "*Send us victorious*" before an extra big sea came bursting across and washed them off the deck—every man but one of the pair beneath the poop—and *he* dropped his hold before the next wave; being stunned, I reckon. The others went out of sight at once, but the trumpeter—being, as I said, a powerful man as well as a tough swimmer—rose like a duck, rode out a couple of breakers, and came in on the crest of the third. The folks looked to see him broke like an egg at their feet; but when the smother cleared, there he was, lying face downward on a ledge below them; and one of the men that happened to have a rope round him—I forget the fellow's name, if I ever heard it—jumped down and grabbed him by the ankle as he began to slip back. Before the next big sea, the pair were hauled high enough to be out of harm, and another heave brought them up to grass. Quick work; but master trumpeter wasn't quite dead; nothing worse than a cracked head and three staved ribs. In twenty minutes or so they had him in bed, with the doctor to tend him.

'Now was the time—nothing being left alive upon the transport—for my father to tell of the sloop he'd seen driving upon the Manacles. And when he got a hearing, though the most were set upon salvage, and believed a wreck in the hand, so to say, to be worth half a dozen they couldn't see, a good few volunteered to start off with him and have a look. They crossed Lowland Point; no ship to be seen on the Manacles, nor anywhere upon the sea. One or two was for calling my father a liar. "Wait till we come to Dean Point," said he. Sure enough, on the far side of Dean Point, they found the sloop's mainmast washing about with half a dozen men lashed to it—men in red jackets—every mother's son drowned and staring; and a little farther on, just under the Dean, three or four bodies cast up on the shore, one of them a small drummer-boy, side-drum and all; and near by, part of a ship's gig, with "*H.M.S. Primrose*" cut on the stern-board. From this point on, the shore was littered thick with wreckage and dead bodies—the most of them Marines in uniform; and in Godrevy Cove, in particular, a heap of furniture from the captain's cabin, and amongst it a water-tight box, not much damaged, and full of papers, by which when it came to be examined next day, the wreck was easily made out to be the *Primrose*, of eighteen guns, outward bound from Portsmouth, with a fleet of transports for the Spanish War—thirty sail, I've heard, but I've never heard what became of them. Being handled by merchant skippers, no doubt they rode out the gale and reached the Tagus safe and sound. Not but what the captain of the *Primrose* (Mein was his name) did quite right to try and club-haul his vessel when he found himself under the land: only he never ought to have got there if he took proper soundings. But it's easy talking.

'The *Primrose*, sir, was a handsome vessel—for her size, one of the handsomest in the King's service—and newly fitted out at Plymouth Dock. So the boys had brave pickings from her in the way of brass-work, ship's instruments, and the like, let alone some barrels of stores not much spoiled. They loaded themselves with as much as they could carry, and started for home, meaning to make a second journey before the preventive men got wind of their doings and came to spoil the fun. But as my father was passing back under the Dean, he happened to take a look over his shoulder at the bodies there. "Hullo," says he, and dropped his gear, "I do believe there's a leg moving!" And, running fore, he stooped over the small drummer-boy that I told you about. The poor little chap was lying there, with his face a mass of bruises and his eyes closed: but he had shifted one leg an inch or two, and was still breathing. So my father pulled out a knife and cut him free from his drum—that was lashed on to him with a double turn of Manilla rope—and took him up and carried him along here, to this very room that we're sitting in. He lost a good deal by this, for when he went back to fetch his bundle the preventive men had got hold of it, and were thick as thieves along the foreshore; so that 'twas only by paying one or two to look the other way that he picked up anything worth carrying off: which you'll allow to be hard seeing that he was the first man to give news of the wreck.

'Well, the inquiry was held, of course, and my father gave evidence; and for the rest they had to trust to the sloop's papers, for not a soul was saved besides the drummer-boy, and he was raving in a fever, brought on by the cold and the fright. And the seaman and the five troopers gave evidence about the loss of the *Despatch*. The tall trumpeter, too, whose ribs were healing, came forward and kissed the Book; but somehow his head had been hurt in coming ashore; and he talked foolish-like, and 'twas easy seen he would never be a proper man again. The others were taken up to Plymouth, and so went their ways; but the trumpeter stayed on in Coverack; and King George, finding he was fit for nothing, sent him down a trifle of a pension after a while—enough to keep him in board and lodging, with a bit of tobacco over.

'Now the first time that this man—William Tallifer, he called himself—met with the drummer-boy, was about a fortnight after the little chap had bettered enough to be allowed a short walk out of doors, which he took, if you please, in full regimentals. There never was a soldier so proud of his dress. His own suit had shrunk a brave bit with the salt water; but into ordinary frock an' corduroys he declared he would not get—not if he had to go naked the rest of his life; so my father, being a good-natured man and handy with the needle, turned to and repaired damages with a piece or two of scarlet cloth cut from the jacket of one of the drowned Marines. Well, the poor little chap chanced to be standing, in this rig-out, down by the gate of Gunner's Meadow, where they had buried two score and over of his comrades. The morning was a fine one, early in March month; and along came the cracked trumpeter, likewise taking a stroll.

'"Hullo!" says he; "good mornin'! And what might you be doin' here?"

'"I was a-wishin'," says the boy, "I had a pair o' drum-sticks. Our lads were buried yonder without so much as a drum tapped or a musket fired; and that's not Christian burial for British soldiers."

'"Phut!" says the trumpeter, and spat on the ground; "a parcel of Marines!"

'The boy eyed him a second or so, and answered up: "If I'd a tab of turf handy, I'd bung it at your mouth, you greasy cavalryman, and learn you to speak respectful of your betters. The Marines are the handiest body of men in the service."

'The trumpeter looked down on him from the height of six foot two, and asked: "Did they die well?"

'"They died very well. There was a lot of running to and fro at first, and some of the men began to cry, and a few to strip off their clothes. But when the ship fell off for the last time, Captain Mein turned and said something to Major Griffiths, the commanding officer on board, and the Major called out to me to beat to quarters. It might have been for a wedding, he sang it out so cheerful. We'd had word already that 'twas to be parade order, and the men fell in as trim and decent as if they were going to church. One or two even tried to shave at the last moment. The Major wore his medals. One of the seamen, seeing I had hard work to keep the drum steady—the sling being a bit loose for me and the wind what you remember—lashed it tight with a piece of rope; and that saved my life afterwards, a drum being as good as a cork until 'tis stove. I kept beating away until every man was on deck; and then the Major formed them up and told them to die like British soldiers, and the chaplain read a prayer or two—the boys standin' all the while like rocks, each man's courage keeping up the other's. The chaplain was in the middle of a prayer when she struck. In ten minutes she was gone. That was how they died, cavalryman."

'"And that was very well done, drummer of the Marines. What's your name?"

'"John Christian."

'"Mine is William George Tallifer, trumpeter, of the 7th Light Dragoons—the Queen's Own. I played '*God Save the King*' while our men were drowning. Captain Duncanfield told me to sound a call or two, to put them in heart; but that matter of '*God Save the King*' was a notion of my own. I won't say anything to hurt the feelings of a Marine, even if he's not much over five-foot tall; but the Queen's Own Hussars is a tearin' fine regiment. As between horse and foot, 'tis a question o' which gets the chance. All the way from Sahagun to Corunna 'twas we that took and gave the knocks—at Mayorga and Rueda, and Bennyventy." (The reason, sir, I can speak the names so pat is that my father learnt 'em by heart afterwards from the trumpeter, who was always talking about Mayorga and Rueda and Bennyventy.) "We made the rear-guard, under General Paget, and drove the French every time; and all the infantry did was to sit about in wine-shops till we whipped 'em out, an' steal an' straggle an' play the tom-fool in general. And when it came to a stand-up fight at Corunna, 'twas the horse, or the best part of it, that had to stay sea-sick aboard the transports, an' watch the infantry in the thick o' the caper. Very well they behaved, too: 'specially the 4th Regiment, an' the 42nd Highlanders an' the Dirty Half-Hundred. Oh, ay; they're decent regiments, all three. But the Queen's Own Hussars is a tearin' fine regiment. So you played on your drum when the ship was goin' down? Drummer John Christian, I'll have to get you a new pair o' drum-sticks for that."

'Well, sir, it appears that the very next day the trumpeter marched into Helston, and got a carpenter there to turn him a pair of box-wood drum-sticks for the boy. And this was the beginning of one of the most curious friendships you ever heard tell of. Nothing delighted the pair more than to borrow a boat off my father and pull out to the rocks where the *Primrose* and the *Despatch* had struck and sunk; and on still days 'twas pretty to hear them out there off the Manacles, the drummer playing his tattoo—for they always took their music with them—and the trumpeter practising calls, and making his trumpet speak like an angel. But if the weather turned roughish, they'd be walking together and talking; leastwise, the youngster listened while the other discoursed about Sir John's campaign in Spain and Portugal, telling how each little skirmish befell; and of Sir John himself, and General Baird and General Paget and Colonel Vivian, his own commanding officer, and what kind of men they were; and of the last bloody stand-up at Corunna, and so forth, as if neither could have enough.

'But all this had to come to an end in the later summer; for the boy, John Christian, being now well and strong again, must go up to Plymouth to report himself. 'Twas his own wish (for I believe King George had forgotten all about him), but his friend wouldn't hold him back. As for the trumpeter, my father had made an arrangement to take him on as a lodger as soon as the boy left; and on the morning fixed for the start, he was up at the door here by five o'clock, with his trumpet slung by his side, and all the rest of his kit in a small valise. A Monday morning it was, and after breakfast he had fixed to walk with the boy some way on the road towards Helston, where the coach started. My father left them at breakfast together, and went out to meat the pig, and do a few odd morning jobs of that sort. When he came back, the boy was still at the table, and the trumpeter standing here by the chimney-place with the drum and trumpet in his hands, hitched together just as they be at this moment.

' "Look at this," he says to my father, showing him the lock; "I picked it up off a starving brass-worker in Lisbon, and it is not one of your common locks that one word of six letters will open at any time. There's *janius* in this lock; for you've only to make the rings spell any six-letter word you please, and snap down the lock upon that, and never a soul can open it—not the maker, even—until somebody comes along that knows the word you snapped it on. Now, Johnny here's goin', and he leaves his drum behind him; for, though he can make pretty music on it, the parchment sags in wet weather, by reason of the sea-water getting at it; an' if he carries it to Plymouth, they'll only condemn it and give him another. And, as for me, I shan't have the heart to put lip to the trumpet any more when Johnny's gone. So we've chosen a word together, and locked 'em together upon that; and, by your leave I'll hang 'em here together on the hook over your fireplace. Maybe Johnny'll come back; maybe not. Maybe, if he comes, I'll be dead an' gone, an' he'll take 'em apart an' try their music for old sake's sake. But if he never comes, nobody can separate 'em; for nobody beside knows the word. And if you marry and have sons, you can tell 'em that here are tied together the souls of Johnny Christian, drummer of the Marines, and William George Tallifer, once trumpeter of the Queen's Own Hussars. Amen."

'With that he hung the two instruments 'pon the hook there; and the boy stood up and thanked my father and shook hands; and the pair went forth of the door, towards Helston.

'Somewhere on the road they took leave of one another; but nobody saw the parting, nor heard what was said between them. About three in the afternoon the trumpeter came walking back over the hill; and by the time my father came home from the fishing, the cottage was tidied up and the tea ready, and the whole place shining like a new pin. From that time for five years he lodged here with my father, looking after the house and tilling the garden; and all the while he was steadily failing, the hurt in his head spreading, in a manner, to his limbs. My father watched the feebleness growing on him, but said nothing. And from first to last neither spake a word about the drummer, John Christian; nor did any letter reach them, nor word of his doings.

'The rest of the tale you'm free to believe sir, or not, as you please. It stands upon my father's words, and he always declared he was ready to kiss the Book upon it before judge and jury. He said, too, that he never had the wit to make up such a yarn; and he defied anyone to explain about the lock, in particular, by any other tale. But you shall judge for yourself.

'My father said that about three o'clock in the morning, April fourteenth of the year 'fourteen, he and William Tallifer were sitting here, just as you and I, sir, are sitting now. My father had put on his clothes a few minutes before, and was mending his spiller by the light of the horn lantern, meaning to set off before daylight to haul the trammel. The trumpeter hadn't been to bed at all. Towards the last he mostly spent his nights (and his days, too) dozing in the elbow-chair where you sit at this minute. He was dozing then (my father said), with his chin dropped forward on his chest, when a knock sounded upon the door, and the door opened, and in walked an upright young man in scarlet regimentals.

'He had grown a brave bit, and his face was the colour of wood-ashes; but it was the drummer, John Christian. Only his uniform was different from the one he used to wear, and the figures "38" shone in brass upon his collar.

'The drummer walked past my father as if he never saw him, and stood by the elbow-chair and said:

' "Trumpeter, trumpeter, are you one with me?"

'And the trumpeter just lifted the lids of his eyes, and

answered, "How should I not be one with you, drummer Johnny—Johnny boy? The men are patient. 'Til you come, I count; while you march, I mark time; until the discharge comes."

'"The discharge has come tonight," said the drummer, "and the word is Corunna no longer"; and stepping to the chimney-place, he unhooked the drum and trumpet, and began to twist the brass rings of the lock, spelling the word aloud, so—C-O-R-U-N-A. When he had fixed the last letter, the padlock opened in his hand.

'"Did you know, trumpeter, that when I came to Plymouth they put me into a line regiment?"

'"The 38th is a good regiment," answered the old Hussar, still in his dull voice. "I went back with them from Sahagun to Corunna. At Corunna they stood in General Fraser's division, on the right. They behaved well."

'"But I'd fain see the Marines again," says the drummer, handing him the trumpet; "and you—you shall call once more for the Queen's Own. Matthew," he says, suddenly, turning on my father—and when he turned, my father saw for the first time that his scarlet jacket had a round hole by the breast-bone, and that the blood was welling there—"Matthew, we shall want your boat."

'Then my father rose on his legs like a man in a dream, while they two slung on, the one his drum, and t'other his trumpet. He took the lantern, and went quaking before them down to the shore, and they breathed heavily behind him; and they stepped into his boat, and my father pushed off.

'"Row you first for Dolor Point," says the drummer. So my father rowed them out past the white houses of Coverack to Dolor Point, and there, at a word, lay on his oars. And the trumpeter, William Tallifer, put his trumpet to his mouth and sounded the *Revelly*. The music of it was like rivers running.

'"They will follow," said the drummer. "Matthew, pull you now for the Manacles."

'So my father pulled for the Manacles, and came to an easy close outside Carn dû. And the drummer took his sticks and beat a tattoo, there by the edge of the reef; and the music of it was like a rolling chariot.

'"That will do," says he, breaking off; "they will follow. Pull now for the shore under Gunner's Meadow."

'Then my father pulled for the shore, and ran his boat in under Gunner's Meadow. And they stepped out, all three, and walked up to the meadow. By the gate the drummer halted and began his tattoo again, looking towards the darkness over the sea.

'And while the drum beat, and my father held his breath, there came up out of the sea and the darkness a troop of many men, horse and foot, and formed up among the graves; and others rose out of the graves and formed up—drowned Marines with bleached faces, and pale Hussars riding their horses, all lean and shadowy. There was no clatter of hoofs or accoutrements, my father said, but a soft sound all the while, like the beating of a bird's wing, and a black shadow lying like a pool about the feet of all. The drummer stood upon a little knoll just inside the gate, and beside him the tall trumpeter, with hand on hip, watching them gather; and behind them both my father, clinging to the gate. When no more came, the drummer stopped playing, and said, "Call the roll."

'Then the trumpeter stepped towards the end man of the rank and called, "Troop-Sergeant-Major Thomas Irons!" and the man in a thin voice answered, "Here!"

' "Troop-Sergeant-Major Thomas Irons, how is it with you?"

'The man answered, "How should it be with me? When I was young, I betrayed a girl; and when I was grown up, I betrayed a friend, and for these things I must pay. But I died as a man ought. God save the King!"

'The trumpeter called to the next man, "Trooper Henry Buckingham!" and the next man answered, "Here!"

' "Trooper Henry Buckingham, how is it with you?"

' "How should it be with me? I was a drunkard, and I stole, and in Lugo, in a wine-shop, I knifed a man. But I died as a man should. God save the King!"

'So the trumpeter went down the line; and when he had finished, the drummer took it up, hailing the dead Marines in their order. Each man answered to his name, and each man ended with "God save the King!" When all were hailed, the drummer stepped back to his mound, and called:

' "It is well. You are content, and we are content to join you. Wait yet a little while."

'With this he turned and ordered my father to pick up the

lantern, and lead the way back. As my father picked it up, he heard the ranks of dead men cheer and call, "God save the King!" all together, and saw them waver and fade back into the dark, like a breath fading off a pane.

'But when they came back here to the kitchen, and my father set the lantern down, it seemed they'd both forgot about him. For the drummer turned in the lantern-light—and my father could see the blood still welling out of the hole in his breast—and took the trumpet-sling from around the other's neck, and locked drum and trumpet together again, choosing the letters on the lock very carefully. While he did this he said:

' "The word is no more Corunna, but Bayonne. As you left out an 'n' in Corunna, so must I leave out an 'n' in Bayonne." And before snapping the padlock, he spelt out the word slowly—"B-A-Y-O-N-E." After that, he used no more speech; but turned and hung the two instruments back on the hook; and then took the trumpeter by the arm; and the pair walked out into the darkness, glancing neither to right nor left.

'My father was on the point of following, when he heard a sort of sigh behind him; and there, sitting in the elbow-chair, was the very trumpeter he had just seen walk out by the door! If my father's heart jumped before, you may believe it jumped quicker now. But after a bit, he went up to the man asleep in the chair, and put a hand upon him. It was the trumpeter in flesh and blood that he touched; but though the flesh was warm, the trumpeter was dead.

'Well, sir, they buried him three days after; and at first my father was minded to say nothing about his dream (as he thought it). But the day after the funeral, he met Parson Kendall coming from Helston market: and the parson called out: "Have 'ee heard the news the coach brought down this mornin'?" "What news?" says my father. "Why, that peace is agreed upon." "None too soon," says my father. "Not soon enough for our poor lads at Bayonne," the parson answered. "Bayonne!" cries my father, with a jump. "Why, yes"; and the parson told him all about a great sally the French had made on the night of April 13th. "Do you happen to know if the 38th Regiment was engaged?" my father asked. "Come, now," said Parson Kendall, "I didn't know you was so well up in the campaign. But, as it happens, I *do* know that the 38th was engaged, for 'twas they that held a cottage and stopped the French advance."

'Still my father held his tongue; and when, a week later, he walked into Helston and bought a *Mercury* off the Sherborne rider, and got the landlord of the "Angel" to spell out the list of killed and wounded, sure enough, there among the killed was Drummer John Christian, of the 38th Foot.

'After this, there was nothing for a religious man but to make a clean breast. So my father went up to Parson Kendall and told the whole story. The parson listened, and put a question or two, and then asked:

' "Have you tried to open the lock since that night?"

' "I hadn't dared to touch it," says my father.

' "Then come along and try." When the parson came to the cottage here, he took the things off the hook and tried the lock. "Did he say '*Bayonne*'? The word has seven letters."

' "Not if you spell it with one 'n' as *he* did," says my father.

'The parson spelt it out—B-A-Y-O-N-E. "Whew!" says he, for the lock had fallen open in his hand.

'He stood considering it a moment, and then he says, "I tell you what. I shouldn't blab this all round the parish, if I was you. You won't get no credit for truth-telling, and a miracle's wasted on a set of fools. But if you like, I'll shut down the lock again upon a holy word that no one but me shall know, and neither drummer nor trumpeter, dead or alive, shall frighten the secret out of me."

' "I wish to gracious you would, parson," said my father.

'The parson chose the holy word there and then, and shut the lock back upon it, and hung the drum and trumpet back in their place. He is gone long since, taking the word with him. And till the lock is broken by force, nobody will ever separate those twain.'

THE HOOTING CAIRN

Cairn Kenidzhek, pronounced Kenidjack, signifying Hooting Cairn, is on the north road from St Just to Penzance, and is strikingly distinguished from other hills by its rugged character. Hoary stones, bleached by sunshine of ages, are reared in fantastic confusion. The spirits of the Celts, possibly the spirits of a yet older people, dwell amidst those rocks. Within the shadow of this hill are mounds and barrows, and mystic circles, and holed stones, and rude altars, still telling of the past. The dead hold undisputed possession of all around; no ploughshare has dared to invade this sacred spot, and every effort made by modern man to mark his sway is indicated by its ruin. Nothing but what the Briton planted remains, and, if tales tell true, it is probable long years must pass before the Englishman can banish the Celtic powers who here hold sovereign sway.

ROBERT HUNT

THE MISANTHROPE

J. D. BERESFORD

1

Since I have returned from the rock and discussed the story in all its bearings, I have begun to wonder if the man made a fool of me. In the deeps of my consciousness I feel that he did not. Nevertheless, I cannot resist the effect of all the laughter that has been evoked by my narrative. Here on the mainland the whole thing seems unlikely, grotesque, foolish. On the rock the man's confession carried absolute conviction. The setting is everything; and I am, perhaps, thankful that my present circumstances are so beautifully conducive to sanity. No one appreciates the mystery of life more than I do; but when the mystery involves such a doubt of oneself, I find it pleasanter to forget. Naturally, I do not want to believe the story. If I did I should know myself to be some kind of human horror. And the terror of it all lies in the fact that I may never know precisely what kind . . .

Before I went we had eliminated the facile and banal explanation that the man was mad, and had fallen back upon the two inevitable alternatives: Crime and Disappointed Love. We were human and romantic, and we tried desperately hard not to be too obvious.

Once before a man had made the same attempt and had built or tried to build a house on the Gulland rock; but he had been defeated within a fortnight, and what was left of his building was taken off the Island and turned into a tin church. It is there still. We all went to Trevone and ruminated over and round it, perhaps with some faint hope that one of us might, all-unknowingly, have the abilities of a psychometrist.

Nothing came of that visit but a slight intensification of those theories that were already becoming a little stale. We compare the early failure of thirty years ago, the attempt that was baffled, with the present success. For this new misanthrope had lived on the Gulland through the whole winter —and still lived. Indeed, the fact of his presence on that awful lump of rock was now accepted by the country people; to them he was scarcely a shade madder than the other visitors; that remunerative, recurrent host that this year broke their journey to Bedruthan in order to stand on Trevone beach and stare foolishly at the just visible hut that stuck like a cubical gall on the landward face of that humped, desolate island.

We all did that; stared at nothing in particular and meditated enormously; but in what I felt at the time was a wild spirit of adventure, I went out one night to the point of Gunver Head and saw an actual light within that distant hut; a patch of golden lichen on the mother parasite.

Some aspect of humanity I found in that light it was that finally decided me; that and some quality of sympathy, perhaps with the hermit—mad, criminal, or lovelorn?—who had found sanctuary from the pestilent touch of the encroaching crowd. It was, in fact, a wildish night, and I stayed until the little yellow speck went out, and all I could see through the murk was an occasional canopy of curving spray when the elbow of the Trevose Light touched a bare corner of that black Gulland.

The making of a decision was no difficult matter, but while I waited for the necessary calm that would permit the occasional boat to land provisions on the island two miles out from the mainland, I suffered qualms of doubt and nervousness. And I suffered them alone, for I had determined that no hint of my adventure should be given to anyone of our party until the voyage had been made. They might think that I had gone fishing, an excuse which had all the air of probability given to it by the coming of the boatman to say that the tide and wind would serve that morning. I had warned—and bribed—him to give no clue to my friends of the goal of my proposed excursion.

My nervousness suffered no decrease as we approached the rock and saw the authentic figure of its single inhabitant awaiting our arrival. I had some consolation in the thought that he would be in some way prepared by the sight of our surprisingly passengered boat; but my mind shuddered at the necessity for using some conventional form of address if I would make at once my introduction and excuse. The civilised opening was so hopelessly incapable of expressing my sympathy, presenting instead so unmistakably, it seemed to me, the single solution of common curiosity. I wondered that he had not—as the boatman so clearly assured me was the case—had other prying visitors before me.

My self-consciousness increased as we came nearer to the single opening among the spiked rocks, that served as a miniature harbour at half-tide. I felt that I was being watched by the man who now stood awaiting us at the water's edge. And suddenly my spirit broke, I decided that I could not force myself upon him, that I would remain in the boat while its cargo was delivered, and then return with the boatmen to Trevone. So resolute was I in this plan that when we had pulled in to the tiny landing-place, I kept my gaze steadfastly averted from the man I had come to see, and stared solemnly out at the humped back of Trevose, seen now in an entirely new aspect.

The sound of the hermit's voice startled me from a perfectly genuine abstraction.

'Fairly decent weather today,' he remarked with, I thought, a touch of nervousness. He had, I remembered, addressed the same remark to the boatmen, who were now conveying their cargo up to the hut.

I looked up and met his stare. He was, indeed, regarding me with a curious effect of concentration, as if he were eager to note every detail of my expression.

'Jolly,' I replied. 'Been pretty beastly the last day or two. Kept you rather short, hasn't it?'

'I make allowances for that,' he said. 'Keep a reserve, you know. Are you staying over there?' He nodded towards the bay.

'For a week or two,' I told him, and we began to discuss the country around Harlyn with the eagerness of two strangers who find a common topic at a dull reception.

'Never been on the Gulland before, I suppose?' he ventured at last, when the boatmen had discharged their load and were evidently ready to be off.

'No, no, I haven't,' I said, and hesitated. I felt that the invitation must come from him.

He boggled over it by saying, 'Dashed awkward place to get to, and nothing to see, of course. I don't know if you're at all keen on fishing?'

'Rather,' I said with enthusiasm.

'There's deep water on the other side of the rock,' he

went on. 'In the right weather you get splendid bass there.' He stopped and then added, 'It'll be absolutely top hole for 'em, this afternoon.'

'Perhaps I could come back . . .' I began; but the boatman interrupted me at once.

'Yew can coom back tomorrow, sure 'nough,' he said. 'Tide only serves wance avery twalve hours.'

'If you'd care to stay, now . . .' began the hermit.

'Thanks! it's awfully good of you. I should like to of all things,' I said.

I stayed on the clear understanding that the boatmen were to fetch me the next morning.

II

At first there was really very little that seemed in any way strange about the man on the Gulland. His name, he told me, was William Copley, but it appeared that he was no relation to the Copleys I knew. And if he had shaved he would have looked a very ordinary type of Englishman roughing it on a holiday. His age I judged to be between thirty and forty.

Only two things about him struck me as a little queer during our very successful afternoon's fishing. The first was that intense appraising stare of his, as if he tried to fathom the very depths of one's being. The second was an inexplicable devotion to one particular form of ceremony. As our intimacy grew, he dropped the ordinary formal politeness of a host; but he insisted always on one observance that I supposed at first to be the merely conventional business of giving precedence.

Nothing would induce him to go in front of me. He sent me ahead even as we explored the little purlieus of his rock—the only level square yard on the whole island was in the floor of the hut. But presently I noticed that this peculiarity went still further, and that he would not turn his back on me for a single moment.

That discovery intrigued one. I still excluded the explanation of madness—Copley's manner and conversation were so convincingly sane. But I reverted to and elaborated those other two suggestions that had been made. I could not avoid the inference that the man must in some strange way be afraid of me; and I hesitated as to whether he were flying from some form of justice or from revenge, perhaps a vendetta. Either theory seemed to account for his intense, appraising stare. I inferred that his longing for companionship had grown so strong that he had determined to risk the possibility of my being an emissary, sent by some—to me—exquisitely romantic person or persons who desired Copley's death. I recalled, and wallowed in, some of the marvellous imaginings of the novelist. I wondered if I could make Copley speak by convincing him of my innocent identity. How I thrilled at the prospect!

But the explanation of it all came without any effort on my part.

He sent me out of the hut while he prepared our supper—quite a magnificent meal, by the way. I saw his reason at once; he could not manage all that business of cooking and laying the table without turning his back on me. One thing, however, puzzled me a little; he drew down the blind of the little square window as soon as I had gone outside.

Naturally, I made no demur. I climbed down to the edge of the sea—it was a glorious evening—and waited until he called me. He stood at the door of the hut until I was within a few feet of him, and then retreated into the room and sat down with his back to the wall.

We discussed our afternoon's sport as we had supper, but when we had finished and our pipes were going, he said, suddenly:

'I don't see why I shouldn't tell you.'

Like a fool, I agreed eagerly, when I might so easily have stopped him. . . .

'It began when I was quite a kid,' he said. 'My mother found me crying in the garden; and all I could tell her was that Claude, my elder brother, looked "horrid." I couldn't bear the sight of him for days afterwards, either; but I was such a perfectly normal child that they weren't seriously perturbed about this one idiosyncrasy of mine. They thought that Claude had "made a face" at me, and frightened me. My father whacked me for it eventually.

'Perhaps that whacking stuck in my mind. Anyway, I didn't confide my peculiarity to anyone until I was nearly seventeen. I was ashamed of it, of course. I am still—in a way.'

He stopped and looked down, pushed his plate away from him, and folded his arms on the table. I was pining to ask a question, but I was afraid to interrupt. And after a moment's hesitation he looked up and held my gaze again, but now without that inquiring look of his. Rather, he seemed to be looking for sympathy.

'I told my house-master,' he said. 'He was a splendid chap, and he was very decent about it; took it all quite seriously and advised me to consult an oculist, which I did. I went in the holidays with the pater—I had given him a more reasonable account of my trouble—and he took me to the best man in London. He was tremendously interested, and it proves that there must be something in it, that it can't be imagination, because he really found a defect in my eyes, something quite new to him, he said. He called it a new form of astigmatism; but, of course, as he pointed out, no glasses would be any use to me.'

'But what . . . ?' I began, unable to keep down my curiosity any longer.

Copley hesitated, and dropped his eyes. 'Astigmatism, you know,' he said, 'is a defect—I quote the dictionary. I learned that definition by heart; I often puzzle over it still—"causing images of lines having a certain direction to be indistinctly seen, while those of lines transverse to the former are distinctly seen." Only mine is peculiar in the fact that my sight is perfectly normal except when I look back at anyone over my shoulder.' He looked up, almost pathetically. I could see that he hoped I might understand without further explanation.

I had to confess myself utterly mystified. What had this trifling defect of vision to do with his coming to live on the Gulland, I wondered.

I frowned my perplexity. 'But I don't see . . .' I said.

He knocked out his pipe and began to scrape the bowl with his pocket-knife. 'Well, mine is a kind of moral astigmatism, too,' he said. 'At least, it gives me a kind of moral insight. I'm afraid I must call it insight. I've proved in some cases that . . .' He dropped his voice. He was apparently deeply engrossed in the scraping out of his pipe. He kept his eyes on it as he continued.

'Normally, you understand, when I look at people straight

in the face, I see them as anybody else sees them. But when I look back at them over my shoulder I see . . . oh! I see all their vices and defects. Their faces remain, in a sense the same, perfectly recognisable, I mean, but distorted—beastly. . . . There was my brother Claude—good-looking chap, he was—but when I saw him . . . that way . . . he had a nose like a parrot, and he looked sort of weakly voracious . . . and vicious.' He stopped and shuddered slightly, and then added: 'And one knows, now, that he is like that, too. He's just been hammered on the Stock Exchange. Rotten sort of failure it was. . . .

'And then Denison, my house-master, you know; such a decent chap. I never looked at him, that way, until the end of my last term at school. I had got into the habit, more or less, of never looking over my shoulder, you see. But I was always getting caught. That was an instance. I was playing for the School against the Old Boys. Denison called out, "Good luck, old chap," just as I was going in, and I forgot and looked back at him. . . .'

I waited, breathless, and as he did not go on, I prompted him with 'Was he . . . "wrong" too?'

Copley nodded. 'Weak, poor devil. His eyes were all right, but they were fighting his mouth, if you know what I mean. There would have been an awful scandal at the school there, four years after I left, if they hadn't hushed it up and got Denison out of the country.

'Then, if you want any more instances, there was the oculist—big, fine chap, he was. Of course, he made me look at him over my shoulder, to test me. He asked me what I saw, and I told, more or less. He was simply livid for a moment. He was a sensualist, you see; and when I saw him that way he looked like some filthy old hog.

'The thing that really finished me,' he went on, after a long interval, 'was the breaking off of my engagement to Helen. We were frightfully in love with one another, and I told her about my trouble. She was very sympathetic, and I suppose rather sentimentally romantic, too. She believed it was some sort of spell that had been put on me. I think, anyway, she had a theory that if I once saw anybody truly and ordinarily over my shoulder, I should never have any more trouble—the spell-would-be-broken sort of thing. And, of course, *she* wanted to be the person. I didn't resist her much. I was infatuated, I suppose. Anyway, I thought she was perfection and that it was simply impossible that I could find any defect in her. So I agreed, and looked—that way. . . .'

His voice had fallen to an even note of despondency, as though the telling of this final tragedy in his life had brought him to the indifference of despair. 'I looked,' he continued, 'and saw a creature with no chin and watery, doting eyes; a faithful, slobbery thing—eugh! I can't . . . I never spoke to her again. . . .

'That broke me, you know,' he said presently. 'After that I didn't care. I used to look at everyone that way, until I had to get away from humanity. I was living in a world of beasts. Most of them looked like some beast or bird or other. The strong were vicious and criminal; and the weak were loathsome. I couldn't stick it. In the end—I had to come here away from them all.'

A thought occurred to me. 'Have you ever looked at yourself in the glass?' I asked.

He nodded. 'I'm no better than the rest of them,' he said. 'That's why I grew this rotten beard. I hadn't got a looking-glass here.'

'And you can't keep a stiff neck, as it were,' I asked, 'going about looking humanity straight in the face?'

'The temptation is too strong,' Copley said. 'And it gets stronger. Curiosity, partly, I suppose; but partly it's the momentary sense of superiority it gives you. You see them like that, you know, and forget how you look yourself. And then after a bit it sickens you.'

'You haven't . . .' I said, and hesitated, I wanted to know, and yet I was horribly afraid. 'You haven't,' I began again, 'er—you haven't—er—looked at me yet . . . that way?'

'Not yet,' he said.

'Do you suppose . . . ?'

'Probably. You look all right, of course. But then so did heaps of the others.'

'You've no idea *how* I should look to you, that way?'

'Absolutely none. I've been trying to guess, but I can't.'

'You wouldn't care . . . ?'

'Not now,' he said sharply. 'Perhaps, just before you go.'

'You feel fairly certain, then . . . ?'

He nodded, with disgusting conviction.

I went to bed, wondering whether Helen's theory wasn't a true one; and if I might not break the spell for poor Copley.

III

The boatmen came for me soon after eleven next morning. I had shaken off some of the feeling of superstitious horror that had held me overnight, and I had not repeated my request to Copley; nor had he offered to look into the dark places of my soul.

He came down after me to the landing-place and we shook hands warmly, but he said nothing about my revisiting him.

And then, just as we were putting off, he turned back towards the hut and looked at me over his shoulder—just one quick glance.

'Wait,' I commanded the boatmen, and I stood up and called to him.

'I say, Copley,' I shouted.

He turned and looked at me, and I saw that his face was transfigured. He wore an expression of foolish disgust and loathing, I had seen something like it on the face of an idiot child who was just going to be sick.

I dropped down into the boat and turned my back on him.

I wondered then if that was how he had seen himself in the glass.

But since I have only wondered what it was he saw in me. . . .

And I can never go back to ask him.

ARISE, TUCKER

On the bleak road between Helston and Wendron Churchtown, at its highest and wildest spot, three roads meet about a quarter of a mile from the latter place. Here, at 'Three Cross,' as the place is called, years ago, when the Downs were unenclosed (it being more desolate then than it is even now), a poor suicide named 'Tucker' was buried. Few liked to pass up Row's Lane, leading there, after nightfall; for Tucker's shade had more than once been seen. One man, however, valiant in his cups, on his return from Helston market, cracked his whip and shouted lustily, 'Arise, Tucker,' as he passed the place. It is said Tucker did arise, and fixed himself on the saddle behind the man as he rode on horseback, and accompanied him—how far it is not said. This was often repeated, until the spirit, becoming angry, refused any more to quit his disturber, and continued to trouble him, till 'Parson Jago' was called in to use his skill, which was effectual, in 'laying' Tucker's spirit to rest.

ROBERT HUNT

THE BOTATHEN GHOST

R. S. HAWKER

There was something very painful and peculiar in the position of the clergy in the west of England throughout the seventeenth century. The Church of those days was in a transitory state, and her ministers, like her formularies, embodied a strange mixture of the old belief with the new interpretation. Their wide severance also from the great metropolis of life and manners, the city of London (which in those times was civilized England, much as the Paris of our own day is France), divested the Cornish clergy in particular of all personal access to the master-minds of their age and body. Then, too, the barrier interposed by the rude rough roads of their country, and by their abode in wilds that were also inaccessible, rendered the existence of a bishop rather a doctrine suggested to their belief than a fact revealed to the actual vision of each in his generation. Hence it came to pass that the Cornish clergyman, insulated within his own limited sphere, often without even the presence of a country squire (and unchecked by the influence of the Fourth Estate—for until the beginning of this nineteenth century, *Flindell's Weekly Miscellany*, distributed from house to house from the pannier of a mule, was the only light of the West), became developed about middle life into an original mind and man, sole and absolute within his parish boundary, eccentric when compared with his brethren in civilized regions, and yet, in German phrase, 'a whole and seldom man' in his dominion of souls. He was 'the parson', in canonical phrase—that is to say, The Person, the somebody of consequence among his own people. These men were not, however, smoothed down into a monotonous aspect of life and manners by this remote and secluded existence. They imbibed, each in his own peculiar circle, the hue of surrounding objects, and were tinged into a distinctive colouring and character by many a contrast of scenery and people. There was the 'light of other days', the curate by the sea-shore, who professed to check the turbulence of the 'smugglers' landing' by his presence on the sands, and who 'held the lantern' for the guidance of his flock when the nights were dark, as the only proper ecclesiastical part he could take in the proceedings. He was soothed and silenced by the gift of a keg of hollands or a chest of tea. There was the merry minister of the mines, whose cure was honeycombed by the underground men. He must needs have been artist and poet in his way, for he had to enliven his people three or four times a year, by mastering the arrangements of a 'guary', or religious mystery, which was duly performed in the topmost hollow of a green barrow or hill, of which many survive, scooped out into vast amphitheatres and surrounded by benches of turf which held two thousand spectators. Such were the historic plays, *The Creation* and *Noe's Flood*, which still exist in the original Celtic as well as the English text, and suggest what critics and antiquaries these Cornish curates, masters of such revels, must have been—for the native language of Cornwall did not lapse into silence until the end of the seventeenth century. Then, moreover, here and there would be one parson more learned than his kind in the mysteries of a deep and thrilling lore of peculiar fascination. He was a man so highly honoured at college for natural gifts and knowledge of learned books which nobody else could read, that when he 'took his second orders' the bishop gave him a mantle of scarlet silk to wear upon his shoulders in church, and his lordship had put such power into it that, when the parson had it rightly on, he could 'govern any ghost or evil spirit', and even 'stop an earthquake'.

Such a powerful minister, in combat with supernatural visitations, was one Parson Rudall, of Launceston, whose existence and exploits we gather from the local tradition of his time, from surviving letters and other memoranda, and indeed from his own 'diurnal' which fell by chance into the hands of the present writer. Indeed, the legend of Parson Rudall and the Botathen Ghost will be recognized by many Cornish people as a local remembrance of their boyhood.

It appears, then, from the diary of this learned master of the grammar school—for such was his office as well as perpetual curate of the parish—'that a pestilential disease did break forth in our town in the beginning of the year A.D. 1665; yea, and it likewise invaded my school, insomuch that therewithal certain of the chief scholars sickened and died'. 'Among others who yielded to the malign influence was Master John Eliot, the eldest son and the worshipful heir of Edward Eliot, Esquire, of Trebursey, a stripling of sixteen years of age, but of uncommon parts and hopeful ingenuity. At his own especial motion and earnest desire I did consent to preach his funeral sermon.' It should be remembered here that, howsoever strange and singular it may sound to us that a mere lad should formally solicit such a performance at the hands of his master, it was in consonance with the habitual usage of those times. The old services for the dead had been abolished by law, and in the stead of sacrament and ceremony, month's mind and year's mind, the sole substitute which survived was the general desire 'to partake', as they called it, of a posthumous discourse, replete with lofty eulogy and flattering remembrance of the living and the dead. The diary proceeds:

'I fulfilled my undertaking, and preached over the coffin in the presence of a full assemblage of mourners and lachrymose friends. An ancient gentleman, who was then and there in the church, a Mr Bligh, of Botathen, was much affected by my discourse, and he was heard to repeat to himself certain parentheses therefrom, especially a phrase from Maro Virgilius, which I had applied to the deceased youth, "*Et puer ipse fuit cantari dignus.*"

'The cause wherefore this old gentleman was moved by my applications was this: He had a first-born and only son—a child who, but a very few months before, had been not unworthy the character I drew of young Master Eliot, but who, by some strange accident, had of late quite fallen away from his parent's hopes, and become moody, and sullen, and distraught. When the funeral obsequies were over, I had no sooner come out of church than I was accosted by this aged parent, and he besought me incontinently, with a singular energy, that I would resort with him forthwith to his abode at Botathen that very night; nor could I have delivered myself from his importunity, had not Mr Eliot urged his claim to enjoy my company at his own house. Hereupon I got loose, but not until I had pledged a fast assurance that I would pay him, faithfully, an early visit the next day.'

'The Place', as it was called, of Botathen, where old Mr Bligh resided, was a low-roofed, gabled manor-house of the fifteenth century, walled and mullioned, and with clustered chimneys of dark-grey stone from the neighbouring quarries of Ventor-gan. The mansion was flanked by a pleasance or enclosure in one space, of garden and lawn, and it was surrounded by a solemn grove of stag-horned trees. It had the sombre aspect of age and solitude, and looked the very scene of strange and supernatural events. A legend might well belong to every gloomy glade around, and there must surely be a haunted room somewhere within its walls. Hither, according to his appointment, on the morrow, Parson Rudall betook himself. Another clergyman, as it appeared, had been invited to meet him, who, very soon after his arrival, proposed a walk together in the pleasance, on the pretext of showing him, as a stranger, the walks and trees, until the dinner-bell should strike. There, with much prolixity, and with many a solemn pause, his brother minister proceeded to 'unfold the mystery'.

A singular infelicity, he declared, had befallen young Master Bligh, once the hopeful heir of his parents and of the lands of Botathen. Whereas he had been from childhood, a blithe and merry boy, 'the gladness', like Isaac of old, of his father's age, he had suddenly, and of late, become morose and silent—nay, even austere and stern—welling apart, always solemn, often in tears. The lad had at first repulsed all questions as to the origin of this great change, but of late he had yielded to the importune researches of his parents, and had disclosed the secret cause. It appeared that he resorted every day, by a pathway across the fields, to this very clergyman's house, who had charge of his education, and grounded him in the studies suitable to his age. In the course of his daily walk he had to pass a certain heath or down where the road wound along through tall blocks of granite with open spaces of grassy sward between. There, in a certain spot, and always in one and the same place, the lad declared that he encountered, every day, a woman with a pale and troubled face, clothed in a long loose garment of frieze, with one hand always stretched forth, and the other pressed against her side. Her name, he said, was Dorothy Dinglet, for he had known her well from his childhood, and she often used to come to his parents' house; but that which troubled him was, that she had now been dead three years, and he himself had been with the neighbours at her burial; so that, as the youth alleged, with great simplicity, since he had seen her body laid in the grave, this that he saw every day must needs be her soul or ghost. 'Questioned again and again,' said the clergyman, 'he never contradicts himself; but he relates the same and the simple tale as a thing that cannot be gainsaid. Indeed, the lad's observance is keen and calm for a boy of his age. The hair of the appearance, sayeth he, is not like anything alive, but it is so soft and light that it seemeth to melt away while you look; but her eyes are set, and never blink—no, not when the sun shineth full upon her face. She maketh no steps, but seemeth to swim along the top of the grass; and her hand, which is stretched out alway, seemeth to point at something far away, out of sight. It is her continual coming; for she never faileth to meet him, and to pass on, that hath quenched his spirits; and although he never seeth her by night, yet he cannot get his natural rest.'

'Thus far the clergyman; whereupon the dinner-clock did sound, and he went into the house. After dinner, when young Master Bligh had withdrawn with his tutor, under excuse of their books, the parents did forthwith beset me as to my thoughts about their son. Said I, warily, "The case is strange but by no means impossible. It is one that I will study, and fear not to handle, if the lad will be free with me, and fulfil all that I desire." The mother was overjoyed, but I perceived that old Mr Bligh turned pale, and was downcast with some thought which, however, he did not express. Then they bade that Master Bligh should be called to meet me in the pleasance forthwith. The boy came, and he rehearsed to me his tale with an open countenance, and, withal, a pretty modesty of speech. Verily he seemed *ingenui vultus puer ingenuique pudoris*. Then I signified to him my purpose. "Tomorrow," said I, "we will go together to the place; and if, as I doubt not, the woman shall appear, it will be for me to proceed according to knowledge, and by rules laid down in my books." '

The unaltered scenery of the legend still survives, and, like the field of the forty footsteps in another history, the place is still visited by those who take interest in the supernatural tales of old. The pathway leads along a moorland waste, where large masses of rock stand up here and there from the grassy turf, and clumps of heath and gorse weave their tapestry of golden and purple garniture on every side. Amidst all these, and winding along between the rocks, is a natural footway worn by the scant, rare tread of the village traveller. Just midway, a somewhat larger stretch than usual of green sod expands, which is skirted by the path, and which is still identified as the legendary haunt of the phantom, by the name of Parson Rudall's Ghost.

But we must draw the record of the first interview between the minister and Dorothy from his own words. 'We met,' thus he writes, 'in the pleasance very early, and before any others in the house were awake; and together the lad and myself proceeded towards the field. The youth was quite composed, and carried his Bible under his arm, from whence he read to me verses, which he said he had lately picked out, to have always in his mind. These were Job vii. 14, "Then thou scarest me with dreams, and terrifiest me through visions"; and Deuteronomy xxviii. 67, "In the morning thou shalt say, Would God it were even! and at even thou shalt say Would to God it were morning; for the fear of thine heart wherewith thou shalt fear, and for the sight of thine eyes which thou shalt see."

'I was much pleased with the lad's ingenuity in these pious applications, but for mine own part I was somewhat anxious and out of cheer. For aught I knew this might be a *dæmonium meridianum*, the most stubborn spirit to govern and guide that any man can meet, and the most perilous withal. We had hardly reached the accustomed spot, when we both saw her at once gliding towards us; punctually as the ancient writers describe the motion of their "lemures, which swoon along the ground, neither marking the sand nor bending the herbage". The aspect of the woman was exactly that which had been related by the lad. There was the pale and stony face, the strange and misty hair, the eyes firm and fixed, that gazed, yet not on us, but on something that they saw far, far away; one hand and arm stretched out, and the other grasping the girdle of her waist. She floated along the field like a sail upon a stream, and glided past the spot where we stood, pausingly. But so deep was the awe that overcame me, as I stood there in the light of day, face to face with a human soul separate from her bones and flesh, that my heart and purpose both failed me. I had resolved to speak to the spectre in the appointed form of words, but I did not. I stood like one amazed and speechless, until she had passed clean out of sight. One thing remarkable came to pass. A spaniel dog, the favourite of young Master Bligh, had followed us, and lo! when the woman drew nigh, the poor creature began to yell and bark piteously, and ran backward and away, like a thing dismayed and appalled. We returned to the house, and after I had said all that I could to pacify the lad, and to soothe the aged people, I took my leave for that time, with a promise that when I had fulfilled certain business elsewhere, which I then alleged, I would return and take orders to assuage these disturbances and their cause.

'*January 7, 1665*.—At my own house, I find, by my books, what is expedient to be done; and then *Apage, Sathanas*!

'*January 9, 1665*.—This day I took leave of my wife and family, under pretext of engagements elsewhere, and made my secret journey to our diocesan city, wherein the good and venerable bishop then abode.

'*January 10*.—*Deo gratias*, in safe arrival in Exeter; craved and obtained immediate audience of his lordship; pleading it was for counsel and admonition on a weighty and pressing cause; called to the presence; made obeisance; then and by command stated my case—the Botathen perplexity—which I moved with strong and earnest instances and solemn asseverations of that which I had myself seen and heard. Demanded by his lordship, what was the succour that I had come to entreat at his hands. Replied, licence for my exorcism, that so I might, ministerially, allay this spiritual visitant, and thus render to the living and the dead release from this surprise. "But," said our bishop, "on what authority do you allege that I am entrusted with faculty so to do? Our Church, as is well known, hath abjured certain branches of her ancient power, on grounds of perversion and abuse." "Nay, my lord," I humbly answered, "under favour, the seventy-second of the canons ratified and enjoined on us, the clergy anno Domini 1604, doth expressly provide, that 'no minister, *unless he hath* the licence of his diocesan bishop, shall essay to exorcize a spirit, evil or good'. Therefore it was," I did here mildly allege, "that I did not presume to enter on such a work without lawful privilege under your lordship's hand and seal." Hereupon did our wise and learned bishop, sitting in his chair, condescend upon the theme at some length with many gracious interpretations from ancient writers and from Holy Scriptures, and I did humbly rejoin and reply, till the upshot was that he did call in his secretary and command him to draw the aforesaid faculty, forthwith and without further delay, assigning him a form, insomuch that the matter was incontinently done; and after I had disbursed into the secretary's hands certain moneys for signitary purposes, as the manner of such officers hath always been, the bishop did himself affix his signature under the *sigillum* of his see, and deliver the document into my hands. When I knelt down to receive his benediction, he softly said, "Let it be secret, Mr R. Weak brethren! weak brethren!"'

This interview with the bishop, and the success with which he vanquished his lordship's scruples, would seem to have confirmed Parson Rudall very strongly in his own esteem, and to have invested him with that courage which he evidently lacked at his first encounter with the ghost.

The entries proceed: '*January 11, 1665.—Therewithal* did I hasten home and prepare my instruments, and cast my figures for the onset of the next day. Took out my ring of brass, and put it on the index-finger of my right hand, with the *scutum Davidis* traced thereon.

'*January 12, 1665.*—Rode into the gateway at Botathen, armed at all points, but not with Saul's armour, and ready. There is danger from the demons, but so there is in the surrounding air every day. At early morning then, and alone—for so the usage ordains—I betook me towards the field. It was void, and I had thereby due time to prepare. First I paced and measured out my circle on the grass. Then I did mark my pentacle in the very midst, and at the intersection of the fire angles I did set up and fix my crutch of raun (rowan). Lastly, I took my station south, at the true line of the meridian, and stood facing due north. I waited and watched for a long time. At last there was a kind of trouble in the air, a soft and rippling sound, and all at once the shape appeared, and came on towards me gradually. I opened my parchment-scroll, and read aloud the command. She paused, and seemed to waver and doubt; stood still; then I rehearsed the sentence again, sounding out every syllable like a chant. She drew near my ring, but halted at first outside, on the brink. I sounded again, and now at the third time I gave the signal in Syriac—the speech which is used, they say, where such ones dwell and converse in thoughts that glide.

'She was at last obedient, and swam into the midst of the circle, and there stood still, suddenly. I saw, moreover, that she drew back her pointing hand. All this while I do confess that my knees shook under me, and the drops of sweat ran down my flesh like rain. But now, although face to face with the spirit, my heart grew calm, and my mind was composed. I knew that the pentacle would govern her, and the ring must bind, until I gave the word. Then I called to mind the rule laid down of old, that no angel or fiend, no spirit, good or evil, will ever speak until they have been first spoken to. *N.B.*—This is the great law of prayer. God Himself will not yield reply until man hath made vocal entreaty, once and again. So I went on to demand, as the books advise; and the phantom made answer, willingly. Questioned wherefore not at rest. Unquiet, because of a certain sin. Asked what, and by whom. Revealed it; but it is *sub sigillo*, and therefore *nefas dictu*; more anon. Inquired, what sign she could give that she was a true spirit and not a false fiend. Stated, before next Yule-tide a fearful pestilence would lay waste the land and myriads of souls would be loosened from their flesh, until, as she piteously said, "our valleys will be full." Asked again, why she so terrified the lad. Replied: "It is the law: we must seek a youth or a maiden of clean life, and under age, to receive messages and admonitions." We conversed with many more words, but it is not lawful for me to set them down. Pen and ink would degrade and defile the thoughts she uttered, and which my mind received that day. I broke the ring and she passed, but to return once more next day. At evensong, a long discourse with that ancient transgressor, Mr B. Great horror and remorse; entire atonement and penance; whatsoever I enjoin; full acknowledgement before pardon.

'*January 13, 1665.*—At sunrise I was again in the field. She came in at once, and, as it seemed, with freedom. Inquired if she knew my thoughts, and what I was going to relate? Answered, "Nay, we only know what we perceive and hear; we cannot see the heart." Then I rehearsed the penitent words of the man she had come up to denounce, and the satisfaction he would perform. Then said she,

"Peace in our midst." I went through the proper forms of dismissal, and fulfilled all as it was set down and written in my memoranda; and then, with certain fixed rites, I did dismiss that troubled ghost, until she peacefully withdrew, gliding towards the west. Neither did she ever afterward appear, but was allayed until she shall come in her second flesh to the valley of Armageddon on the last day.'

These quaint and curious details from the 'diurnal' of a simple-hearted clergyman of the seventeenth century appear to betoken his personal persuasion of the truth of what he saw and said, although the statements are strongly tinged with what some may term the superstition, and others the excessive belief, of those times. It is a singular fact, however, that the canon which authorizes exorcism under episcopal licence is still a part of the ecclesiastical law of the Anglican Church, although it might have a singular effect on the nerves of certain of our bishops if their clergy were to resort to them for the faculty which Parson Rudall obtained. The general facts stated in his diary are to this day matters of belief in that neighbourhood; and it has been always accounted a strong proof of the veracity of the Parson and the Ghost that the plague, fatal to so many thousands, did break out in London at the close of that very year. We may well excuse a triumphant entry, on a subsequent page of the 'diurnal', with the date of July 10, 1665; 'How sorely must the infidels and heretics of this generation be dismayed when they know that this Black Death, which is now swallowing its thousands in the streets of the great city, was foretold six months agone, under the exorcisms of a country minister, by a visible and suppliant ghost! And what pleasures and improvements do such deny themselves who scorn and avoid all opportunity of intercourse with souls separate, and the spirits, glad and sorrowful, which inhabit the unseen world!'

THE PHANTOM SHIP

In the midst of the dreary waste of Goonhilly, which occupies a large portion of the Lizard promontory, is a large piece of water known as 'Croft Pasco Pool', where it is said at night the form of a ghostly vessel may be seen floating with lug-sails spread. A more dreary, weird spot could hardly be selected for a witches' meeting; and the Lizard folk were always—a fact—careful to be back before dark, preferring to suffer inconvenience rather than risk the sight of the ghostly lugger.

ROBERT HUNT

ALL SOULS' NIGHT

A. L. ROWSE

They were sitting—the Dean and two of his colleagues—in the quiet of a summer evening upon the terrace of that college, that quadrangle which gives you a panorama of the spire of St Mary's, with its gathered pinnacles clustered at the base, the light and classical elegance of Aldrich's spire of All Saints in the background, the bulky Roman magnificence of the Radcliffe Camera in the foreground, and away to the innumerable crockets and finials of the Bodleian Library. It was that hour of summer evening when the late light lit up the clock upon the northern face of St Mary's tower: a rare and disturbing thing to the hearts of those few whose attention was caught by it. Somehow it brought home to them, in an inexpressible way, the feeling of the transcendence of things, the mutability of the temporal order, the immutability of the eternal.

Nine was striking upon all the brazen tongues of the clocks of Oxford. There was the old-lady-stepping-up-stairs chime of New College that began the clamour, followed by the lugubrious descent and ascent of St Mary's like going down into the tomb. Last of all, the deliberate, suspensive, velvety boom of Tom from Christ Church.

> Midnight has come, and the great Christ Church bell
> And many a lesser bell sound through the room;
> And it is All Souls' Night . . .

the words ran through the dreamy mind of the young English don, while his attention wandered from the desultory conversation the Dean was having with his senior colleague, the Classic.

The Fellows had had their coffee in the open air, so warm was the evening. And now, replete, at leisure, these three were enjoying the evening air, the Classic his pipe, the Dean his cigar. When the youngest of them next attended, his colleague was asking the Dean:

'By the way, what was it that overtook young Colenso?

I remember he was a lad of considerable promise as an undergraduate—great things were expected of him when he was elected to his Fellowship. I never really rightly understood what came of him. I dare say you know, my dear Dean: wasn't he one of your West-Country clientèle?'

This was the regular phrase with which they teased the Dean about the interest he took, the almost fatherly interest, in the long file of young men coming up to the University from the West Country, from scholarship candidates to D.Phil. researchers. Anybody of West-Country connections had a claim upon his attention, if not upon his affections.

'Well, in a manner of speaking, he was,' said the Dean. Then, after a pause, unhurriedly savouring his cigar, turning it round on his lips:

'There was no mystery about it, you know. It is quite clear what happened.' He laid emphasis upon 'what happened' as if there were some mystery *before* what had happened.

'Poor fellow, he's still alive, though in a bad way, I gather.'

(A ghost may come;

—mused the abstracted, ruminating mind of the young English don—

For it is a ghost's right,
His element is so fine
Being sharpened by his death,
To drink from the wine-breath
While our gross palates drink from the whole wine.

But it wasn't the poor fellow of the Dean's acquaintance who was the ghost, he reflected. Perhaps he had seen a ghost? He sat up and began to attend in earnest.)

'No, there was no mystery attached to it,' the Dean was saying. 'But it was certainly a very curious story.

'You see, I knew the lad—or rather the part of Cornwall he comes from—well. His was a sweet nature, a charming disposition; and very level-headed and sensible, too. He was the last person you would have expected to—' He paused to inspect the end of his cigar, to see if it were properly alight.

'Expected to what?' said the eager young Fellow, a little tense.

The Dean took no notice, went on his unhurried way. 'He had got here on his own steam, won a lot of scholarships. He was quite capable of looking after himself. He hadn't much of a family in the background. I believe there was a father, who had gone off to America, or something of the sort, leaving the mother to fend for herself. The lad was brought up largely by his sister, who was much older than he was, ten or fifteen years. She was more of a mother to him.

'Up here young Colenso (Tristam was his name: rather curious, too—I believe it ran in the family), well, he did very well, got his first and was elected to a Research Fellowship almost at once. Perhaps it was rather a rush, a bit too much for him; it may have overtaxed his strength. Better that these things should come slowly—let them ripen in due season,' said the Dean, who had had several set-backs in his early academic career and thought it a good principle for everybody else that things should not come to them too easily.

'But he had to get something, poor lad,' he added kindly. 'And he had a very good subject for research right on his own doorstep, so to speak. You know the old Cornish family, the Lantyans, of Carn Tyan, who were the greatest landowners in Cornwall in the Middle Ages—though they have lost a good deal of their property there since. They were absentees from the county for a long time, from the sixteenth century to the eighteenth. They were Catholics, and during the years of Elizabeth's war with Spain they were not allowed to live in so dangerous an area, so remote from the centre, so near the sea, and with the sympathies of their peasantry all Catholic like their own. It was for them a prohibited area—as for strangers today. How little things change in human affairs!' (The Dean enjoyed a good ripe platitude as it might be a peach or a nectarine.) 'Well, the Lantyans have gone on being Catholic in an unbroken tradition—and very proud they are of the fact. They say that in their chapel at Carn Tyan there is a lamp that has never been allowed to go out since the Reformation.

'The old Lady Lantyan bore an extraordinary character in those parts. Jane Lucinda: she was the last representative of the Blanchminsters who owned a great deal of land in North Cornwall in the Middle Ages, and also one half, the secular half, of the Scilly Islands. The old lady was a regular termagant, a well-known character all over the West Country. For one thing she had a terrific temper; was immensely family-proud and haughty; a dominating old woman who lived to be ninety and led her household and servants and everybody near her the devil of a life. Particularly, for some odd reason, her chaplains. She seemed to hate them; she certainly persecuted them. Yet it never occurred to her to dispense with them: there always had been a priest in the household, and she simply couldn't conceive of a house without one—for her. It may be that she wanted somebody or something to torment. She had no children. Her husband had died years before, leaving her in control of the money. So she remained on in possession, keeping her heir, an elderly cousin of her husband's, at arm's length. He couldn't have afforded to dispossess her anyway; he was entirely dependent on her for what would, or might, come to him after her death.

'So she lived on at Carn Tyan, tormenting priests her chief pleasure in life, you might say. One after the other they left her, driven to distraction. One poor man, the last of them, a French priest, a cultivated, quiet, melancholy sort of man, who already seemed to have enough on his mind—as if there was a something in the background—was driven over the edge. He became stark raving mad. To begin with, she starved them. It wasn't that she was mean. It was just that she had very odd views about diet. She lived on next to nothing herself, with the aid—it is true—of the very best old cognac, such as she had a good store of in her cellars. You never come across brandy like that nowadays.' The Dean gave a heartfelt sigh.

'The old lady was immensely aristocratic; she couldn't believe but what suited her very well must be good for everybody else. She fed her priests mostly on rice and currants, relieved with brandy at every meal to wash it down. She insisted that to keep your health you had to drink brandy five times a day. Such of them as survived the endless rice and currant puddings became hopeless topers on the brandy. The combination was too much for her last priest. But then he had something else on his mind.

'Not that that much worried the old tartar, Jane Lucinda. Protest after protest at her treatment of her priests had been made by her bishop, the Bishop of Lysistrata. Without the slightest effect. At last a writ of excommunication was made out to be served upon her. Did that defeat her? Not a bit of it. On the threshold of ninety, she called for her carriage and at once drove off to a Carmelite convent the other side of the county, to enter upon a long retreat, leaving instructions that on no account should any correspondence be forwarded. So that the writ never reached her. When the bishop at length learned where she was, she left for the house of a relation in Worcestershire. By the time it reached Worcestershire she was in London. For the bishop it was a regular wild-goose chase, making him look ridiculous in the eyes of the whole Catholic community who knew perfectly well what was going on. I believe the old termagant thoroughly enjoyed the last months of her life. Having outwitted her ecclesiastical superiors, she took to her bed at her town house in London and died still officially at peace with the Church, and fortified with all the accustomed rites.

'At last her cousin, the thirteenth baronet—an elderly man of sixty—entered into possession of the almost derelict estate, a great house in which nothing had been changed since the eighteen-sixties. He was the last of the family. Like many another bachelor who had himself done nothing to keep going the succession, he was interested in his family history. And on coming into possession, he found a muniment room stuffed full of old deeds and documents, letter-books and papers, and wanted some help in going through them. This is where young Tristam Colenso came in. Sir Richard had heard of his expertise in deciphering medieval handwritings, and the idea was that he should write a family history of the Lantyans and Blanchminsters. After all, the least the baronet could do for posterity, since he hadn't produced any issue of his own to continue it—so far as we are aware; at any rate not any legitimate issue,' the Dean added cautiously.

'So young Colenso was invited down for a week-end to take a preliminary look through the papers in the muniment room. It was his first experience of stopping in a great country house—and alas, poor lad, I suppose it will be his last. He was very excited and impressed. All very natural. He had heard of Carn Tyan all his life, but had never so much as set eyes on it.

'The house is in a very remote and un-get-at-able part

of Cornwall—the Tamar Valley. Also one of the most lovely, with a singular fascination of its own. You know, my dear Done, how people up here are liable to say, "Of course the coast of Cornwall is very beautiful, but the county has no interior." What nonsense it is!' The Dean, a very patriotic Cornishman, grew quite angry. 'Just the impression of ignorant tourists rushing through the county along the main motor-road to Newquay or St Ives or the Lizard. As a matter of fact, all the river valleys are extremely beautiful country: Helford, the country of the Fal, the Fowey, the Camel, and not least, the Tamar. In spite of Plymouth being at its gate, the Tamar country is the most unspoiled, as it is the least accessible.'

Having made his point, the Dean sent the junior Fellow into the smoking-room to get him a whisky-and-soda, and on his return resumed the story. Meanwhile they watched the last rosy flush of light catching the topmost cupola of the Radcliffe Camera. The Dean's colleague, the Classic, thought of the lovely orange-and-rose flush in the sky of Rome as you look from the Pincio Gardens to the dome of St Peter's in the west across the darkening spaces of the city. Yes, he thought, the Camera is the most Roman thing in Oxford—and as good as anything in Rome. Fortified by his whisky-and-soda, the Dean resumed.

'When Colenso arrived at the station at Launceston after an all-day journey, there was a car to meet him. They drove for miles through the failing light—it was the very beginning of November—until he recognised the long serrated crest of the woods, the nearest he had ever been to the house, upon the next ridge. It was not without a thrill that he passed through the gates, the pillars surmounted by lions upholding shields, the arms of the Lantyans, and into the grand gloom of the park. He just caught sight of the splendid fans of the cedars upon the lawn when they drove up to the front door.

'His first impression was of the magnificence of the great double staircase which swept down its marble arms into the hall. He was shown up to his room by a maid carrying a little hand lamp through the vast and shadowy gloom. At the head of the staircase there were at least eight great mahogany doors in a semicircle. They went through one on the right and along an unfinished corridor, through several large rooms, of which one was a book-room, and down a little curved passage to his own door. It opened into a huge state-bedroom, with great state-bed under a canopy at the farther end. His heart sank a little at the spectacle: it was altogether too grand for him, he thought. He felt that it was a mistake, his coming.

'Opening a note the maid had given him, he found that it was from Sir Richard, regretting that he couldn't be there to receive him. He had had to go urgently into Plymouth that afternoon and hoped to be back in time for dinner at eight. Tristam had plenty of time to look round and dress at leisure. He was evidently expected to occupy this room: there was a wood fire lit for him in the Adam fireplace. It burnt up cheerfully. But the room was far too large to be cheerful in itself. Fancy sleeping in a bedroom that had a couple of columns at each end, thought Tristam; in a state-bed large enough for four. How does one sleep in it? he wondered; does one sleep on the outer edge, or leap boldly into the middle?

'He looked round by the light of the lamp and the candles lighted on the dressing-table. No electricity anywhere. The room gave an impression of the gloomy splendour of a former age, rather than of opulence in this. There were eighteenth-century portraits on the wall, and beautiful things about: silver candlesticks on dressing-table and writing-table, and a smaller one for the hand with snuffers beside the bed. All very well, he thought, but no electric light to turn on, if you should want it in the night.

'With time on his hands he settled down to write the journal-letter that he wrote to his sister when anything special happened to him, such as going away on a visit. Then it was time for him to change. He put on his newly starched shirt and trousers and silk socks, arranged his studs and cuff-links, when he discovered that he had forgotten to bring a dress tie. The kind of accident that happens to us all, when we are young,' said the Dean sympathetically, with a memory of some similar misadventure to himself before he had lost his youthful diffidence. 'And what upsets us far worse than many things in themselves more important.

'Tristam was struck with horror. He had specially packed everything himself that morning so that nothing of the kind should happen. Young and inexperienced, he regarded this in the light of a major disaster. It took him a long time to summon up courage to ring the bell. It took an even longer time for the maid to answer his summons from somewhere in the depths of this vast, silent house. She came back with an old-fashioned tie of Sir Richard's, with his compliments.

'As the hour of eight approached he took his lamp and made his way back, not without some doubt and a few wrong turnings, to the head of the magnificent staircase, and downstairs. Going under the arch into the small dining-room he saw a figure in a corner strenuously engaged in drawing a cork. He took him to be the butler. It was in fact Sir Richard, acting as butler himself.

'They shook hands and went into the dining-room together. Tristam was rather set at ease by the unexpected manner of their meeting, was made to feel completely at home by the way Sir Richard chaffed him about the tie—he said it was what he always did himself when *he* was young; the young man ended by being quite conquered by his host's old-fashioned charm of manner. The baronet was very tall and good-looking, with crisp grey hair; in spite of a gouty leg, he would himself get up to fetch Tristam a cigarette or ash-tray, or open the door. Sir Richard certainly knew how to render himself agreeable to the young scholar. During dinner there was a good deal of amusement at the expense of the departed dowager and her ways—fantastic stories of which Sir Richard had a whole repertoire. ('She had her revenge, in her own way,' commented the Dean.) 'Tristam concluded that if the redoubtable Jane Lucinda were after an Elizabethan pattern, haughty and overbearing, like the famous Bess of Hardwick or Lettice Knollys, her successor was the perfection of eighteenth-century courtesy, easy and affable.

'The meal was very simple; there was only one maid to wait at table. The baronet did his own butling. Though the silver was beautiful, Tristam couldn't but observe that the carpet was threadbare. Dinner ended with a couple of glasses of port from the bottle that Sir Richard had been caught in the act of decanting. He took it as a joke and made fun of his impoverished estate. None the less it was evident what a pride he had in his ancestry and everything that concerned his family's history. Tristam could hardly keep up with his references to the seventh or tenth Sir Richard or the heiresses who had brought in this or that estate in the distant past, or his way of thinking of English history as episodes in the more continuous and certain story of his family.

'After dinner, taking their light with them, they went out and down through a stone passage to the muniment room. It was a young researcher's paradise. So many cupboards and presses and chests of drawers, boxes and trunks and iron deed-boxes, crammed full of old documents—most of them medieval, it seemed. There were rent-rolls and accounts, copies of inquisitions, terriers and fines, duplicates of wills, letters and letter-books—all in the most agreeable confusion. Many a day's pleasant work for a couple of enthusiastic antiquarians. But the box which most tickled Tristam's intuitive sense as a researcher—his nose for documents: a sort of sixth sense—was locked and the key lost. Nothing would induce it to open. They tried all the keys, but none would fit the lock. It was most provoking, for from the lettering outside Tristam could see that it contained documents relating to the most interesting of Cornish monastic houses. He tried various little keys of his own upon the lock, but only succeeded in breaking them and leaving their heads in the wards.

'It was after eleven when they gave up, and Sir Richard accompanied his guest up the grand staircase to his room. The fire was burning brightly, throwing elongated shadows across the high ceiling. Tristam got into bed, keeping to the edge of it; there was an interminable space unoccupied the other side of him, he thought. He was surprised at the bed's comfort. He put out his light and tried to settle himself to sleep. But there was still the firelight and those long wavering shadows like fingers pointing across the room at him. Whether it was the port, or the excitement of the muniment room, his head was in a whirl. He was just falling asleep, when the thought of Lady Lantyan's French priest came into his mind. He had gone mad in this house, perhaps in this very room.

'After that, there was no sleep for Tristam. He lay there for a bit, his heart beating audibly beneath the bedclothes of the great bed, listening, straining his ears to catch every sound in the vast silence, an owl hooting outside in the park, the swish-swish—what was it?—of the twigs of a tree against the window-pane. Unable to bear it any longer, unable to sleep, he lit his candle, got out, put on his dressing-gown, and went to the writing-table to take refuge in the comfort of writing to his sister.

'It was the worst thing he could have done, probably; writing only heated his imagination the more, stimulated his nervous sensibility, made him doubly aware of every sound and movement.

'I don't quite know what happened next; one can only piece it together from his account of that night afterwards. He was never very sure of the order in which things happened, even at his best. And, of course—at the worst—' The Dean paused, finished his whisky-and-soda, and went on:

'It seems that he was looking for something to read, something to take back to bed with him. I don't know whether there were any books in the room; he may have gone out through the little passage into the book-room to find something. Or he may have found it in the drawer of that writing-table. Wherever it was, with the unfailing flair of the born researcher—which he undoubtedly had, poor fellow—he put his hand on a little manuscript book that had belonged to the French priest.'

The Dean stopped and lit a cigarette to keep off the gnats which were beginning to pester him, like a cloud of disagreeable memories that one wants to exorcise.

'That little manuscript book, a sort of diary, gave the clue to the secret of the French priest. He had an irremediable sin upon his conscience, which tormented him and turned his life into agony. Apparently he had been in his early years left with the charge of a small child, a boy, whose parents were his near relations. He regarded this charge with distaste, as a burden upon his career (he was poor and ambitious). In his early years he did the minimum he could for this child, had him placed in an orphanage and barely kept touch with his responsibility. Some dozen or fifteen years later he received a message to come to the bedside of his young relation. The lad was now in a seminary.

'The priest found that his uninteresting charge had grown into a youth, intelligent and of great charm—but, alas, far gone in consumption. Touched to the heart at last, but too late, he remained there with him all through that summer and autumn. Until, in fact, the end. The boy died on All Souls' Day, the second of November.

'Every day for the rest of his life when All Souls' Day came round the priest said a requiem for him. When he came to Carn Tyan, as All Souls'-tide approached, he became more and more plunged into profound gloom. An inconsolable misery seemed to possess him, turning him inwards upon himself. During that period he was in the habit of inflicting on himself austerities, which left him in a mingled state of physical exhaustion and mental excitement. It was really the first symptoms of his madness. He thought himself responsible for the death of his young charge. This was his retribution.

'As Tristam picked up the threads of this story of suffering and penance, this confession of guilt from a dead man, something of the priest's state of morbid excitement communicated itself to him. He was already in a very susceptible condition: the strangeness of the house, the excitement of the muniments, the listening silences of the great room in which sleep was now impossible.

'The fire had burned down to a last occasional flicker, making more absolute the shadows in all the room, save for the patch of light by the bedside.

'What was that that stirred at the farther end of the room? Tristam listened with every nerve in his body on edge. In the confusion of his senses he could not tell whether it was something that registered itself to the sense of sight or hearing. He sat up, listening, peering between the great bed-posts into the darkness. The sound came more distinctly from that direction: it was something like a low moan. He listened: the strange hoarse sibilance became clearer: it was a pattern, a mutter of words. But the words did not seem to make sense.

'At last Tristam caught quite distinctly the words, "mea culpa, mea culpa, mea maxima culpa", uttered with an inexpressible anguish such as he thought no human voice could attain. Tristram wasn't a Catholic; he had been brought up an Anglican, a rather High Church Anglican. He recognised the Confession of the priest at the beginning of the Canon of the Mass. The Latin words were spoken with an unmistakable French accent.

'With all his senses alive, his nerves on edge, he watched intently: it was as if he saw everything in the room at once, out of the corners of his eyes. Sitting up in bed looking straight before him to the other end of the room, upon which his fears were concentrated, he suddenly saw the great door behind him at *this* end of the room open softly, slowly on its hinges, as if for someone to pass through. He was transfixed there, waiting. Nobody. Nobody passed through. The great door closed as noiselessly, as slowly as it had opened.

'But was there nobody that had passed through? A sense of unutterable grief, of inconsolable suffering, had invaded the room. It was unnerving. Tristam could stand it no longer.

'Hardly knowing what he was doing, he got out of bed and out of the room at the other end to find himself in darkness outside. His brain was working with the unnatural clarity that goes with such an experience; all his apprehensive senses were aroused by what was about him. He realised, quite rationally, with the disjunctive logic of a dream, that the reason for the curve in the passage leading to the great room was that it was here the end of the chapel abutted on to the house; and he found himself looking down from the family pew high up in the gallery at the west end of the building upon the scene that enacted itself below.

'He had no doubt about what was going on down there. There were the shadowy figures, vested, before the altar; upon the altar itself the two candles of the rubric. Fascinated, unable to move from the spot, he heard the immemorial Roman mutter, the introit of the Mass for the Dead:

Requiem aeternam dona eis, Domine, et lux perpetua
luceat eis.

It seemed to him that he heard the strange toneless voices articulating the *Dies Irae* from the beginning:

Dies irae, dies illa
Solvet saeclum in favilla,
Teste David cum Sibylla

to the very end:

Judicandus homo reus:
Huic ergo parce, Deus.
Pie Jesu, Domine,
Dona eis requiem.

His eyes were so fixed upon the figures round the altar, that it was only when the whimper of the *Dies Irae* was over that he noticed in the gloom before the sanctuary that there was a catafalque, with one taper, no more than a rush-light, burning at the head. It was a small coffin, very slender and shapely. Then he knew whose requiem it was that was proceeding down below.

'With that thought there came over him a sense of inextinguishable grief such as had passed through the great room. Only now it seemed to invade him by every crevice open to its penetration, eyes, ears, mouth, throat. Overwhelmed with a grief that was not his, he stumbled back into the room, lit the candles one by one, every one of them, upon writing-table, dressing-table, at the bedside. If there had been a hundred candles, still he would have lit them all to lighten the oppression weighing upon his spirits.

'He sat down before the dressing-table, face plunged in hands. It was when he removed his hands for a moment that he noticed something strange about his appearance. There were creases, there were lines upon his face, at the corners of mouth and nostrils, around the eyes. It seemed to him that the more he looked, the more lined his face became. It was like the face of someone else. But above all it was the eyes that arrested his attention. His eyes were dark; but the eyes that fixed him in the mirror were grey and steely, with that strange fanatic quality you sometimes see in Frenchmen's eyes. As he watched, the whole face began to twitch: it was the face of a madman.

'In the morning when it was daylight, they found him still seated there before the mirror, gibbering.'

CALLING OF THE DEAD

The fishermen dread to walk at night near those parts of the shore where there may have been wrecks. The souls of the drowned sailors appear to haunt those spots, and the 'calling of the dead' has frequently been heard. I have been told that, under certain circumstances, especially before the coming of storms, or at certain seasons, but always at night, these callings are common. Many a fisherman has declared he has heard the voices of dead sailors 'hailing their own names'.

ROBERT HUNT

THE NARROW WAY

R. ELLIS ROBERTS

I

At his confirmation he had annoyed the Bishop of London (at that time it was Frederick Temple) by insisting on taking the additional names of Alfonso Mary Alexander. He had surprised him by the resolute manner in which he had answered his questions about the origin of taking names at confirmation; and enraged him by his explanation that he desired to be called Alexander in memory of that great Pope, the Lord Alexander VI, who had put the whole Christian world under an obligation by his discovery of the devotion of the Angelus. 'This devotion,' the boy murmured to the astounded Bishop, 'as your Lordship no doubt knows, has been from eternity the privilege of the Holy Angels, and was not entrusted to men until the proximity of the horrible heresies of the German deformation rendered the patronage of Mary necessary for the protection of her son.' The Bishop's chaplain had tried to prevent Frank Lascelles' indiscretion; but Temple's abrupt gesture had hindered his efforts. When Lascelles finished the Bishop gazed at him in silence for a minute.

'Well, I hope you'll live to grow out of this foolery. But you know your rights and you shall have 'em.'

Temple was, as his old foes had discovered years before, eminently just.

More than twenty years had passed since that confirmation. Frank Alfonso Mary Alexander Lascelles had gone to Oxford and to Ely, and had been ordained to a small country parish in that diocese. After two years of his curacy, an injudicious layman presented him to the living of St Uny and St Petroc in the north of Cornwall. He had been there now for over nineteen years. When he had come he found his church empty; now it was full. It was full of children and boys. Occasionally a few mothers, and when he was sober, the village drunkard, and, when she was penitent, the prostitute from the Church Town, came to Mass as well; but generally the Church of St Uny, down by the beach, was filled only by children and boys.

This result Frank Lascelles had been long in attaining. The parish he served was predominantly Methodist. He had found a congregation of three—the publican, the hostler of the hotel, and an old maiden lady who rang the bell, and called herself the pew opener. Lascelles soon shocked the respectability of the publican and the Protestantism of the hostler: but the old lady remained faithful to him. She did not stir when he had the three-decker cut down, and a new altar reared at the East end. She seemed to welcome the great images, Our Lady of the Immaculate Conception, The Sacred Heart, St Joseph and St Anthony which Lascelles put up in his church. She did not care whether he said Mass in Latin or English; and incense and holy water both left her tranquil. It was otherwise with the village. Though the Methodists never entered the church, except for a wedding or a funeral, they thought they had a right to control its services and its priest. There were stormy Easter vestries; there was a Protestant church-warden. One horrible day the fishermen broke into the church and took out the images and threw them down the cliff: by next week new ones were in their places. Lascelles was boycotted by his parishioners, except a few would-be bold spirits; and was outlawed, in the genial English way, by his Bishop; but he stuck at his job, went on saying offices to an empty church, and singing Mass to his pew opener and an occasional visitor. Then after five years or so the change began.

It was not along the usual lines of such changes. Generally priests of Lascelles' religion are eager, masculine people who soon win over the more turbulent elements in the parish, and put them, too, in search of the great adventure of Christianity. But Lascelles, though he had grown up, still remained the boy who had chosen Liguori and Alexander for his patrons. He was obsessed with the reality of the spiritual world, of good and evil. His pillow was wet with the tears he shed for the sins of his parish. He was horrified at the evil of the world, and yet constitutionally unable to defy it in any active way. He had only one strong human affection—and that was a great love for children.

At first this was not reciprocated. His odd figure, his shuffling walk, his stoop and his occasional outbursts of anger produced ridicule and fear rather than love. Then one child somehow found how large the heart of him was; and then another, and then another. He had won the children. But this would have availed him little had it not been for the arrival at St Uny of the Rev. Paul Trengrowse. Mr Trengrowse came to minister to the Primitives about three years after Lascelles' appointment to the parish. He was young, keen, and sincere. He had not been long in the village when the leading members of his congregation told him of the sins of the Parish Priest, and horrors of the parish church. Trengrowse prayed for light. He disliked interfering with the affairs of an alien church; but, if half he was told was true, Lascelles must be fought. So he paid a visit to the church, which was always open, and was duly distressed at the idols he saw there.

As he was gazing at the smirking fatuity of St Anthony, he heard a footstep. It was Lascelles who was coming from the sacristy to the altar. Fortunately, before he began Mass, Lascelles looked down the church and saw 'a congregation.' So he said Mass in English.

Now Trengrowse was no ordinary minister. He was a man of personal holiness, and of real devotion; and that in his spirit which was sincere and mystical recognised in the Popish-seeming priest, muttering his Mass, a kindred soul. Lascelles' absorption in his work, his grave, yet joyful solemnity, his keen sense of the other world made an immense effect on Trengrowse. The Mass proceeded, and when Trengrowse heard 'Therefore with Angels and Archangels and all the Company of Heaven,' he felt that he had had the answer to his prayer. This man was a Christian, however erroneous he might be in details.

So the next Sunday the Primitives, who were hoping for a strong sermon against the Scarlet Woman, were disagreeably surprised. 'Mr Lascelles may be wrong. I think he is wrong, sadly wrong, in many things: but he du love the Lord, and he du worship Him. And, brethren, no man calls Jesus Lord save by the Holy Ghost. Let us pray for Mr Lascelles and the church people of St Uny; and that we may all be led along the narrow way to everlasting life.'

Had Trengrowse been a man of less character he might have failed in his defence of Lascelles. But he was an acceptable preacher, and a man whose plain love of his religion it was impossible to doubt. So, first with grumbling, later with a ready acquiescence, the villagers of St Uny followed his lead.

The result was odd. Lascelles attracted the children more and more; and his services attracted them. This worried Trengrowse not a little; but when one of his congregation said scornfully, 'Those bit games to the church be only fit for babes,' he looked gravely at him and replied, 'Ah! Eli, but the book says, "Unless ye become as little children." ' This silenced Eli, but it did not silence Trengrowse's own heart. How was it Lascelles could do anything with children, a good deal with boys up to fifteen or so, and nothing with men and women, and little with girls? Lascelles' own explanation was simple. His Bishop would not confirm his children until they were thirteen. Lascelles presented them year after year when they were six or seven. He preached an amazing sermon on the three great aids to the Devil in the parish of St Uny —and the three heads of his sermon were: Lust, Hypocrisy and the Lord Bishop. The more respectable of the neighbouring clergy were furious, but the Bishop, who was a simple, humble-minded man (quite unlike to be the ex-head-master who had inducted Lascelles) refused to take any notice of the attack; but also refused to relax his rule about the age of confirmation candidates. The Archdeacon told Lascelles that his parish was the plague-spot of the diocese, and Lascelles retorted that in a mass of corruption any sign of health looks ominous and unusual. But, although he kept up a brave front to the disapprovers, his failure with his people galled him. He would not have minded if they had still been actively hostile. But that had long ceased. They were now fond of their priest. They liked and shared in his notoriety. They supported him against the officials; and when a malicious Protestant from London attempted to stir up a revolt against Lascelles, he was promptly put into the harbour; and Trengrowse started a petition to the Bishop, expressing the affection 'all we, whether church people or Methodists, feel for Mr Lascelles.'

Lascelles' philosophy refused to permit him to see in his failure evidences of his incapacity for his work. He had the proud humility of the perfect priest. Regarding himself as a mere channel for divine grace, he forgot that his personality was so distinctive that it affected the way in which grace reached his people. Once an old friend had tried to make him see this; but the task was hopeless.

'My dear fellow,' said Lascelles, 'I don't see what you mean. All they want is the Gospel. And that I give them. I say Mass for them. I will hear their confessions. I instruct them. I lead their devotions. All beside is mere human embellishment. No doubt a more competent man would be more pleasing to them, but he could do no more than give them the Gospel, could he?'

II

On All Souls' Day, 1912, Lascelles was depressed. Early that morning he had gone up to the cemetery, and said a Requiem in the little chapel. Then there had been the early Mass at 8.30 in church. The church had been full. Not only were all his children there, but there were a good many fathers and mothers: for the services on the day of the dead appealed to a deep human instinct with a power which not even Lascelles could spoil. The *Dies Iræ*, sung in Latin, had sounded oddly from a congregation so predominantly childish: and Lascelles had preached a short sermon on the 'Significance of Death.'

'We exaggerate the importance of death. It is to us death matters, not to the dead. For them it is a release, for us it is a warning. Death of the body is only a symbol. It is death of the soul we must fear. Believe me, it would be worth while for every one of you in this church to die, if by dying, you could bring a soul to Jesus. God knows, I would die for you, if that would bring you. There are those here today—you, Penberthy, and you, Trevose—who have not been to Mass since you were boys. Make a new resolution today, and ask the Holy Souls to help you keep it. Come to your duties, and return to your church.'

Lascelles felt at the time that his appeal lacked force. He knew that after Mass, Penberthy would say to Trevose:

'Bootivul service, bean't it, Tom?'

'Iss—it be that. I du like it for once or twice. But for usual give me the chapel. It be more nat'ral like.'

'Iss—it be. Poor Mr Lascelles, I did think he would have a slap at us.'

'Iss—it be his way. My gosh! I don't mind.'

So Lascelles was depressed. He sat among his books, reading a Renascence treatise on 'Death.' He thought a great deal about death. Sometimes he feared it horribly. It seemed the great enemy of faith. It was so disconcerting a thing, so heartless, so unregarding. At other times he felt defiant. But never did he reach the spirit of St Francis about death. He was too remote from natural life and the events of animal birth and death to understand death as an ordinary thing, something not less usual than the sunset.

'It may be'—he read, 'that there be more deaths than one. For it is evident that some are so hardened in sin that the death of the body comes long after the man has really been dead. Such men are commonly gay and cheerful; for with the death of their soul, has died all godly fear, all apprehension of judgment, all hope of salvation. They become but as brutes. Wherefore the church has always held that heretics, if they be obstinate and beyond recall, may be handed over to the secular arm for the death of the body. It should not trouble us that they display ordinary human virtues: for these be common in the unregenerate, and are but devices of the devil who would persuade men that religion matters naught. They are his children, and may be lawfully treated as such by any godly prince. The church herself kills not: though the Lord Pope, being a Temporal King, has the power of the sword, and may exercise the same.'

Lascelles put the book down and stared at the fire. The words roused a train of thought that almost frightened him. But he was not the man to dismiss any idea because it was terrifying. He believed in giving the devil his due, and always insisted that all temptations should be met boldly, not evaded. He left his chair, and knelt at his prie-dieu, looking at the wounds of the great Crucifix which hung above it.

Half an hour later he rose with a look of resolution on his face.

III

The first case of the plague, as the villagers insisted on calling it, happened just before Epiphany. It attacked Penberthy, who had never been ill before; and in four days he was dead. His disease puzzled the doctor from the market-town, but he put it down as a curious case of infantile paralysis. His colleague from Truro, whom he consulted after the third case had occurred, insisted that the symptoms did not disclose anything more definite than shock following on *status lymphaticus*. The most serious thing was, however, not their incapacity to name, but their inability to cure the mysterious disease which was spreading in St Uny. Except for a general weariness, a disinclination to move, and a curious 'wambling in the innards,' there were no definite symptoms at all to go on. After the second case they had an inquest, but it yielded no results at all, and Dr Marlowe began to talk of getting an expert from London.

It was not until February, however, that any one came. Then by a fortunate chance Sir Joshua Tomlinson came down to St Ives for a holiday. The 'plague' at St Uny had got into the London paper. There had been ten deaths, and two women, the first to be attacked, were lying seriously ill. Dr Marlowe called on Sir Joshua, and the great physician said he would come over and see the patients. Marlowe was glad that chance had sent him a great general physician rather than a surgeon or a specialist. Although he was willing to defy any specialist to find his pet disease in the mysterious sickness that had killed the ten fishermen, he was relieved that no specialist was to be given the opportunity.

'You see, Lascelles,' he said to the priest, 'it's not as if we were in the fifteenth century. We may be in theology, but I'm hanged if we are in medicine. These men are dying like savages: but the savage makes up his mind he has got to die, and dies through sheer hysteria. These fellows want to live. They lust for life.'

'You are right, Marlowe. Their desire for life is a lust. It is scarcely decent in a Christian to cling so to this existence. But there—it's not my business to judge. You know, Marlowe, I have sometimes thought this last month, that this mysterious disease is a judgment on St Uny. It is God's hand held out over our village. Let us pray for those who are dead, and those who are dying, and most of all, dear God, for those who are not yet to die.'

Marlowe, though friendly with Lascelles, was more than a little afraid of him. The vicar had worked like two men during this distress. He had nursed the sick, he had consoled the mourners, he had said Masses and had a service of general humiliation. Somehow he had identified himself with his parish to a degree he had never reached before, and St Uny was grateful to him. But the little doctor was rather afraid. Lascelles was strained and odd in manner. He spent too long a time in prayer, and not long enough at meals or in bed.

'No, Lascelles. I don't agree with you there. Oh! I'm a good Catholic, I hope, and I know God could intervene; but I don't see why He should.'

'No: you don't see why. No one does, Marlowe, until He speaks, and then they are forced to.'

On the Saturday Sir Joshua came over. He saw Mrs Pentreath and Mrs Whichelo, and he shook his head over both of them. He asked them questions about their diet, and about their way of living, while Marlowe stood by, silent and impatient. Then he said a few kindly, cheerful words, and left them in the big room, which the vicar had had fitted up as a hospital ward; for Marlowe thought the cases were better isolated.

'Well, sir, what do you think?'

'What sort of a man is your vicar? He seems liked.'

'Yes—he is. He's an odd chap—a bit mad, I think. A very keen Catholic, and very depressed at his failure to keep the people.'

'Ah! they don't go to church?'

'Well they *do* now. They have done since this damned illness. He's been awfully good to them. And the children have always gone.'

'It's a funny thing, Dr Marlowe, that no child has been ill.'

'Isn't it? That's what I say to young Jones of Truro. He will insist on his shock theory, following on *status lymphaticus*. I keep on pointing out to him that most of the patients are men who have had shocks every week of their lives since they were twelve. They'd have all been dead long since.'

'Yes. I am sure Jones is wrong. But I don't know what this disease is, Dr Marlowe. I suspect, but I don't know.'

'Here is the vicar coming, Sir Joshua. Shall I introduce you?'

'Please do.'

Lascelles was walking rapidly towards them. He looked ill but eager. His eyes were full of a fanatic pleasure, a kind of holy rapture that appeared to make him even taller than he actually was. He acknowledged the introduction with a bow, and would have passed on, but Sir Joshua stopped him with a question.

'You have come from your sick people, Mr Lascelles?'

'Yes. They are no longer sick. I was just in time to hear their confessions, and give them the viaticum.'

'Good God!' Sir Joshua was evidently shocked. 'It's not ten minutes since we left them.'

'No? The end has always been very sudden, hasn't it, Marlowe?'

'Yes. But this is quicker than usual. Do you think, Sir Joshua'—and he lowered his voice—'a post-mortem?'

'No. It would be useless. At least it would be no help to me. By the way, Marlowe, how have you entered the cause of death?'

'Well, sir—I've frankly put "Heart failure, cause unknown." There seemed to be nothing between that and "Act of God."'

'Ah! Marlowe, that's what you should have put,' intervened Lascelles. 'It is the hand of God—the hand of God.' Then, with a bow to Sir Joshua, he hurried away.

'So your vicar thinks it is the hand of God. He may be right. God works through human agents. He is an interesting man, Dr Marlowe.'

'Yes: he is. But this trouble has worried him frightfully. I'm rather nervous for him. Have you got any theory, sir? You talked of suspicion.'

'Well, Dr Marlowe, I'll tell you what I think. Your patients have been murdered.'

Marlowe looked at the great physician, as if he was afraid for his sanity.

'No, Dr Marlowe, I'm not mad, though I have no proof of my assertion. All I ask is this, that I may be allowed to see the next patient within at least half an hour of the beginning of the illness. By the way, can they give me a bed here, do you think? Where do you put up?'

'Oh! I'm staying at the vicar's. I expect he'd be charmed to have you.'

'No. I don't think I will stay with Father Lascelles. I would rather not. I'll find a room somewhere. I think there will be another case tomorrow night.'

IV

That Sunday morning Lascelles preached on the 'Hand of Judgment.' The church was packed. Trengrowse had his service at nine and brought all his congregation to the Mass at eleven. Lascelles seemed wonderfully better. His eye was clearer, his step gayer and his whole figure more buoyant. His tone as he gave out his text was exultant.

'They pierced his hands.

'The symbolism of the Divine Body is strangely arresting. The Jews thought of God as an eye watching, caring for them from heaven. We Christians watch God—here in the Tabernacle, or in the arms of Mary. His care for us we typify by His Hand—the Hand we pierced. This last month God has been with us very wonderfully. He is always with us in the holy Sacrament: but lately He has been with us in the Sacrament of Death. His Hand of Judgment has been over, and under us; it has clasped us—and some of us it has not let go.

'Our natural feeling is one of fear. We are not used to such immediate handling as this of our God's. We have most of us tried to apply religion to our life, now we have to try and apply our life to religion. God will have us think of nothing but Him, speak to none save Him, hope for none save Him. His Hand is still with us. It will bear yet more away from St Uny before we learn our lesson. Let me help you to learn that lesson right. Let us all take care that we renew our trust in God, that we recognise His Hand, that we answer His Love.'

Sir Joshua had listened attentively to Lascelles' sermon. He seemed vaguely disappointed, and he was unwilling to discuss it with Marlowe afterwards. There was no doubt that Lascelles' almost fatalist attitude, while it annoyed the doctor, had a strange welcome from the villagers. They turned in a childlike way to the words of this man who spoke as one who knew the ways and the meaning of the Almighty. Never had Lascelles so much real devotion from his people as he secured during the 'plague.' It was not that they shared his feeling of complete abandonment to the Will of God; but the fact that he had such a feeling made their fates seem more tolerable.

On Sunday evening there was a new case, as Sir Joshua had expected. The disease attacked Mrs Bodilly, the wife of the chief grocer in St Uny. Marlowe was summoned immediately, but he found Sir Joshua already at the poor woman's bedside.

She was frankly terrified; in this her case differed from previous ones, in which the sufferers, though generally resentful, had been not the least afraid. Mrs Bodilly had been at Mass that morning. She had got back and prepared the dinner. At tea-time she had 'felt queer,' but after tea she was better. Then as she was getting ready to go to the special service of Exposition, she fell down and had to be carried up to her room by her husband and sons.

She was, unlike most of the tradesmen's wives, a nominal church woman, but she had never been confirmed and rarely went to church. The fit of external piety roused in her by the 'plague,' was frankly based on nervous alarm. She felt that God was taking it out of St Uny in this way; and she was anxious to escape.

Her illness found her divided between anger and fear. She was angry that her efforts to placate Divine wrath had not been more successful—she was terrified of dying, terrified still more of death as a punishment. In the most desolate way she sought reassurances from Marlowe and Sir Joshua; but neither could give her any certain consolation. The disease presented no different aspects. It indeed presented no aspect at all, except extreme weakness, astonishing slowness of the pulse, and irregular beating of the heart. Although Sir Joshua was there within five minutes of the seizure, he admitted to Marlowe that he could discover nothing of what he suspected.

'I'll be frank, Dr Marlowe, I suspected poison. I still suspect it. I believe all these people have been poisoned in an extremely subtle way by a man so fanatical as to be almost mad. But I can find no trace of the poison. In this case, I will, if you will permit me, conduct a post-mortem, but I expect I shall fail. If I do, I must take my own line, if you wish me to help you.'

'Really, Sir Joshua, you talk more like a detective than a physician.'

'This is a detective's business, Dr Marlowe. I wish it were not.'

Before they left Lascelles arrived. He had been summoned by Mr Bodilly, and he came prepared to give Mrs Bodilly the last rites. As the boy with the light and the bell approached the stairs, Sir Joshua whispered to Marlowe:

'Your vicar seems very certain of her death.'

Marlowe shrugged his shoulders. 'We haven't saved a case, you know.'

The post-mortem yielded no result. That evening Marlowe dined with Sir Joshua at the village inn, and after dinner the great physician told him of his suspicions. Marlowe listened at first angrily, then with an incredulous horror.

'It can't be. The man lives for his parish, I tell you. Why, he would die for it.'

'Yes: I believe he would. Had I found what I looked for, he certainly would.'

'But, my dear sir, there isn't a trace of any known drug. There's no trace of anything.'

'No. I had expected to find—but never mind. I have a great deal of experience, Dr Marlowe, and I am convinced that your vicar has been murdering his parishioners. And tonight I am coming to tell him so. I will walk home with you. You may be present or not, as you please.'

V

Lascelles looked up a little wearily when Sir Joshua had finished speaking.

'Is that all?'

Marlowe intervened.

'Look here, old man—I only came because—you'll forgive me Sir Joshua—I didn't want you to be alone under this monstrous, this fantastic accusation of Sir Joshua's. You've only got to contradict him, and we'll go.'

Lascelles looked gratefully at his friend.

'Thank you, Marlowe. But Sir Joshua is right in telling me his suspicions. You have finished, Sir Joshua?'

'Yes. I should like your explanation if you have one, or your admission of my charge, and your promise that this—this—plague shall cease.'

'You use strange words, sir, for a man who has no evidence for what he says.'

'Yes,'—ejaculated Marlowe, 'yes, by Jove, you do—'

'Please, Marlowe. You will not be content with having

relieved your mind, Sir Joshua. You wish me to answer you?'

'I do. I require it.'

'You know, sir, you great doctors have one failing. It is one priests have too. You cannot avoid talking to me as if I were your patient—a mental, a nervous case. You can't help believing that your firm tone, your almost—may I say it—discourteous manner will impress me. Well, it doesn't.'

Sir Joshua got red. Lascelles' words too entirely diagnosed his method. He was annoyed that he should seem so transparent to a man whom he regarded as at least half-crazy.

'I beg your pardon. There is something in what you say. Men in all professions have their—ah! tricks.'

'Thank you.'

Lascelles got up and stood by the fireplace looking down on his visitor. In the last month he had changed. He seemed bigger and more masculine—more as if he now had personal responsibilities: he looked less of an official, more of a man. He spoke rather slowly.

'You have accused me of murder, Sir Joshua. You ask me to admit my crime, and to promise to cease. Well, I expected your visit. I have long been familiar with your Treatise on Renascence Toxicology: it is as complete as any published book. And I am glad you and Marlowe came tonight. I have my answer ready. I admit nothing and I promise nothing.'

Sir Joshua looked with a puzzled air at the priest. For a moment his accusation seemed a monstrous thing to himself. Then his common sense surged back.

'Father Lascelles, your answer does not satisfy me. I must take other steps.'

'They will not lead anywhere, Sir Joshua. If *you* find no evidence, no other man can. You say my poor people were poisoned. Well, find the poison. Ah—you know you cannot. It is foolish to threaten me. But I will tell you what I had determined to tell Marlowe tonight. First, I do not expect there will be any more deaths from this plague for a long time.

'Secondly, I have a confession to make. Last All Hallows I was depressed. The work here has not gone as it should. I had the children, but not their parents. I thought much of Death and the Departed at that season of all the dead—and at last I prayed to God that if nothing else would move these people, He would send Death. Send Death mysterious and as a judgment. Death has come, and my people have learnt their lesson. All of those who died were reconciled to Holy Church before death. Of those who remain nearly all have adhered to the Church. This afternoon Mr Trengrowse came and asked to be prepared for Confirmation—'

'Trengrowse, the minister—' cried Marlowe.

'And this evening I had notice that all who are competent intend to make their Communion next Sunday. This parish has been won for God, Sir Joshua, and at the cost of thirteen deaths. Isn't it worth it?'

'Father Lascelles, I cannot regard you as sane. You are not only practically admitting your crime, you are disclosing your motives.'

'I beg your pardon, I admit nothing. I acknowledged I prayed to God to visit this people, if necessary, by His secret Death. That is not a crime. Next Sunday I shall tell my people.'

'And have you *prayed* that the deaths shall cease?' asked Sir Joshua ironically.

'I was doing so when you entered,' replied Lascelles quietly.

'Good God, man, your hypocrisy sickens me. You prate of God's intervention, and all the time you've been sending man after man to death by some foul poison of your own.'

'Sir Joshua—do you believe God commonly works without human intervention?'

'Bah! That is sophistry.'

'You condemn the machinery of justice, the compromise of war, our human evasion of rope and guillotine?'

'Surely, Marlowe,' exclaimed Sir Joshua, 'you can't sit and listen quietly to this damnable nonsense?'

Marlowe had been sitting dazed, looking at Lascelles as if he were fascinated. He replied in a remote voice:

'I don't know. I'm wondering'—he gave a nervous laugh—'wondering if Lascelles is a saint or a devil.'

Lascelles went on imperturbably:

'You don't answer me. You can't. Why should you think I, an anointed priest, am less fit to be the door-keeper of death than Lord Justice Ommaney? At least I use no case-law. I am the slave of no precedent. I know my people. I know them individually. I love them as persons. And as persons I judge them.'

The tall figure of the man seemed to glow. His face was lit

with an unnatural beauty, as he stood looking down on the other two, and dared them to answer him.

Sir Joshua rose. He had lost his somewhat pompous judicial air. He was deeply, humanly moved; and he spoke with an anxiety far more impressive than his previous authoritative tone.

'Father Lascelles, I have nothing more to say. I believe you to have done a very horrible, a very wicked thing. I have heard how you would defend yourself if you were legally brought to book for such an offence. Your defence has, as you are aware, no legal force. I think it has no moral force. You are deceiving yourself strangely. One day you will have a great loneliness of heart. You will realize how terrible a responsibility you have taken. Without the sanction of society, without the approval of your church, you have decided alone, the fate of your fellow-creatures. I am sorry for you. Good-night.'

The light left Lascelles' face. He looked suddenly ill and careworn. Then with a high, frantic gesture he flung his hand towards the Crucifix.

'He, too—He, too—was made sin.'

THE HOUR HAS COME...

A fisherman or a pilot was walking one night on the sands at Porth-Towan, when all was still save the monotonous fall of the light waves upon the sand.

He distinctly heard a voice from the sea exclaiming—

'The hour is come, but not the man.'

This was repeated three times, when a black figure, like that of a man, appeared on the top of the hill. It paused for a moment, then rushed impetuously down the steep incline, over the sands, and was lost in the sea.

In different forms this story is told all around the Cornish coast.

ROBERT HUNT

THE PHANTOM HARE

M. H.

'Bessy, did you ever see a white hare?'

'A white hare! No, never. Why do you ask it?'

Susan Stanhope did not say why she asked it. She seemed to have come home in a kind of excitement. I saw her fly up the broad garden path between the beds, crowded with sweet and homely flowers, as though she were in a hurry to escape from some danger. Her light footfall ran up the stairs to our bedroom, where I sat sewing, and she burst upon me with the above question.

'Do not you Cornish people attach some superstition to the appearance of a white hare, Bessy?' she continued. 'I think I once heard mamma say so.'

'Well, I fancy we do, now you speak of it. But I don't know what the superstition is.'

Susan folded the mantle she had taken off, put her bonnet up, and sat down in a chair on the opposite side of the open window. I had drawn my little work-table as close to the window as possible, being anxious to finish mending Janey's frock, which she had torn at the brook stile; and the twilight was already upon us. In September—we were in the earlier days of it—the evenings draw in quickly.

We lived at the Mount Farm, a large estate belonging to the Bertrams, situated near Penryn, in Cornwall. My father, Roger Trenathy, had been born in the parish; his people had rented it for several generations. He was what is called a substantial man, and was superior in cultivation to some farmers; but he lived in a homely style, and we, his children, had to work, as (*he* said) all farmer's daughters ought. Roger was his only son, already as busy on the land as he was. I was the eldest of all; Eunice was next to Roger, and seventeen this summer; little Jane was ten only, and went, day-boarder, to Mrs Pollock's school. A great deal lay upon me, both of work and care. Our two maids were light-headed things, and Eunice was lighter-headed than they were.

Our mother was dead. She had been a clergyman's daughter, and was a true gentlewoman. It was to her training and companionship that I owed all the culture I possessed. Roger was like her: he had her pleasant eyes and her sweet smile. Her only sister had married a clergyman—the Reverend Philip Stanhope. He and his wife had both died, leaving one child, Susan—this same Susan now visiting us. Susan had had a first-rate education, but she had not much fortune: just one thousand pounds in the Three per Cents. When she left school, some eighteen months ago, my father had said she must make her home with us: but she preferred to be independent, and went out as a governess. Moreover, she wrote us word, in a cordial but half-jesting manner, that she should not care to live always in a farm-house. This was the first holiday she had had—seven weeks long it was to be—and she had come to spend it with us, arriving two days ago.

'You found your way readily to Dame Mellon's, Susan?' I asked her, as I stitched away. For she and I were both to have gone to the widow Mellon's cottage after tea, to take the old woman some wool for knitting. For years she had knitted my father's winter stockings—as she did those of many other people around. It was the only work she could do, being blind, and we all liked to employ her. And by the way, though I have called her *old*, she was not yet fifty. Care and illness had served to wrinkle her brow and to bend her back: and we young people are apt to think everybody else old if they have left forty years behind them. But Janey came home with this dreadful rent in her new frock—and the rent went more ways than one. I was angry with her, and had to mend it; and Susan said she would take the wool. So I let her take it, adding a little basket of things from our plentiful larder, and directing her which way to go.

'Oh yes! I found it quite well,' answered Susan. 'It is a picturesque little cottage, resting in that shady dell.'

'What made you ask me about a white hare, Susan?'

'Because I have just seen one. I have had an adventure, Bessy.'

'Indeed! What was it?'

'You were talking yesterday about Miss Bertram,' she said, after a pause, never answering my question—'that she was to marry Mr Arlegh. It was just, you know, as she passed the gate yonder in her pony carriage, drawing an old lady.'

'Her aunt. Well?'

'*Is* she to marry Mr Arlegh?'

'Why, of course she is. They are to be married in November. He is her cousin. Not a first cousin; a second or third. When her father, Sir William, died, thirteen months ago now, the title lapsed, but the Hall and all the large estates were left to Miss Bertram. Upon that, Hubert Arlegh (as is said) hastened to make her an offer, and after a time, but not at first, she accepted him.'

Susan lifted her blue eyes quickly. 'His name is Hubert, is it? What sort of a looking man is he?'

'A very handsome one.'

'Tall and dark?'

'Tall, and rather dark. He is very good-looking indeed.'

'Then I don't think him so, Bessy,' she returned, in a contradictory, positive tone. 'He may be what many people call handsome, as to features and colouring, but he has a most disagreeable expression; and—'

'Why, Susan!' I interrupted. 'What has taken you? Has Mr Arlegh offended you?'

'Offended *me*! Oh dear, no.'

'You spoke like it. Where have you seen him?'

'I will tell you, Bessy. I said I had had an adventure. In coming from Dame Mellon's cottage, through that dark, shady lane that leads from it—I don't know its name—'

'The park lane,' I interrupted. 'It belongs to Miss Bertram's park, but we have the liberty of passing through it.'

'Well, I was coming quickly along, for it seemed to be getting quite dusk there under the trees, swinging the little straw basket in my hand, and doing it so carelessly that it swung off and went ever so many yards beyond me, just as a lady and gentleman turned the corner. I knew her for Miss Bertram—and a nice face I must say she has, and a charming manner. He stooped to pick up the basket, and she said a few pleasant words to me—something to the effect that she could see I had been to Mrs Mellon's cottage, no doubt to take her some good cheer. I did not quite catch them; they were over in a moment, and Mr Arlegh—for I am sure by your description it was he—'

'Yes, yes; no one would be walking with Miss Rose but he: and, for the matter of that, he is the only visitor staying at the Hall. Go on, Susan.'

'At the very moment that he was holding out the basket to me, a beautiful white hare suddenly sprang out of the edge, bounded directly over his feet, and was lost in the opposite bushes. At least, I don't know where else it could have sprung from,' broke off Susan, thoughtfully. 'It seemed to startle him so much that he dropped the basket, and leaped back with a smothered cry. Miss Bertram did not appear to have seen it; she turned her head, and asked what was the matter. "Oh, nothing," he answered lightly, save that he had been careless enough to drop the young lady's basket: but I saw that his face had turned of a ghastly whiteness. As I stooped for the basket, for I was quicker than he, the same white hare reappeared from the bushes, crossed the lane as before, passing over his feet, and was lost to sight in the hedge. Bessy, he shuddered from head to foot like a man in dreadful fear: it is as true as that I am telling it to you.'

'Fear of what?'

'How should I know? Miss Bertram looked about her as though some unseen danger were near, turning her head from side to side. Such was the idea that struck me; but still I do not think she saw the hare. They walked on, wishing me good evening, and I came running all the way home.'

'It must have been a white rabbit, Susan.'

'I assure you it was a hare: I could not mistake it. The question is—Why should it have frightened Mr Arlegh?'

'Another question is,' I said, passing over that, for in truth I saw no solution to it, and thought Susan must be fanciful—'Why this should have made you take a prejudice against Mr Arlegh?'

'It did not make me. It had nothing to do with it. One reason why I do not like him is, that he—'

'That he what, Susan?'

'Well I hardly know how to express it. But he looked at me in so free and ugly a manner. As if really, Bessy, it was just as if I were a "lass o'lightness."'

I was silent. One or two disagreeable stories had gone about to Mr Arlegh's discredit, and people wondered whether they had been quite kept from Miss Bertram. Possibly so; for they were not connected with our immediate neighbourhood, but with his own. He lived near St Huth, a village seven miles off, upon the small property that had been his father's. Rose Bertram's riches, apart from her own sweet self, must have presented a temptation to him. He passed his time chiefly in London before being engaged to Miss Bertram, and made debts there.

'You give that as one reason for taking a dislike to him, Susan, though possibly you were mistaken. What is the other?'

'The other is a private reason of my own, Bessy. I cannot tell it.'

She sat on at the window in deep thought, her blue eyes strangely serious as they gazed outwardly on the gathering gloom, her right hand pushing back unconsciously her fine golden hair. At length, just as it got too dark to see, I made a finish of my work, and we went down to the parlour. Eunice was helping Patience to lay the cloth for supper; father and Roger were coming in for it. Janey had been in bed long ago.

The last thing we did at night was to sing the evening hymn, I or Eunice playing it. Susan offered to play tonight. She was a skilful musician, as compared with us, and her soft touch was of itself melody.

It was Susan's custom to read the psalms for the evening to herself after we got into my bedroom, which she shared with me. On this evening she sat down as usual, but almost immediately closed the prayer-book.

'No, I *cannot* read tonight; it is of no use,' she cried, almost passionately. 'My wandering thoughts will not let me.'

I turned round from the glass, unpinning my collar, and looked at her. Her cheeks were flushed, her eyes wore a troubled light.

'Bessy, will you let me tell you a tale?'

'Certainly I will, dear.'

'Then let us put out the light and sit at the window.'

She clapped the extinguisher on the candle herself, and we sat down at the window—closed now. It was a fine night; the moonlight flooding hill and dale, the bare corn-fields, the pasture lands, and the houses, large and small, scattered among them.

'You know, Bessy, that when mamma died, I was placed at school at Walborough for two years, to complete my education. It was a notedly good school, not a large one, Miss Robertson, the governess, being very indulgent to us. I took a fancy at once to one of the girls. Agnes Garth. She was about my own age, which was sixteen then, and one of the sweetest, best, loveliest girls I ever saw—'

'Lovelier than you?' I interrupted.

'How silly you are!' she exclaimed, laughing and blushing. 'Of course I know that I am—not ugly; but I could not be compared with her. Not but that the girls thought us a little alike, in as much as that we were both fair, with bright complexions and the same coloured hair. They had given her a name, Beauty, and generally called her by it—Beauty Garth. I cannot tell you how I loved that girl: my father and mother were gone, and it seemed that all the love within me was concentrated upon her. She was so gentle, so kind, so good; a very angel.'

I laughed.

'Ah well, it was so, Bessy. Miss Robertson used to say Agnes had no stability, that she might be swayed any way by those she loved; but it was an amiable weakness. We were like sisters all the two years we passed together. She never could think ill of anyone: she put trust in all the world. A sort of cloud hung over her—'

'A cloud?'

'Well, we never could find out who she was. The rest of us talked freely of our home and friends, of our past life; but she was silent as to hers, even to me. An impression obtained in the school—I know not whence derived—that her mother was an actress at a theatre in London. Her father she had never known—that much Agnes did tell us. Miss Robertson never spoke upon the subject: Agnes was treated just as the rest of us were, and we knew nothing.'

'Did she go home for the holidays?'

'No; she passed them at school—as I usually did: and perhaps that served to draw us closer together. My two years were nearly up, when one day, when we were with the German master, Miss Robertson sent in for Agnes; and when the class was over and we got back to the ordinary school-room, we heard that Agnes had gone to London, in answer to some message received by the governess. She came back in a month's time in deep mourning, and told us her mother was dead. But, though her frank spirit was subdued and saddened by the loss, there was evidently some deeper joy within her that had not existed before. I found out what it was—Beauty was in love. She had met a gentleman in London, and was already secretly engaged to him. She would not tell me his name or who he was, though I asked it over and over again. "There will be no necessity for me to be a governess now," she said to me one day—for that's what she was to have been, as her mother left her little, if any, fortune.'

'How old was she, Susan?'

'Eighteen then, just as I was. This was last year, in the earlier part of it. I left the school at Easter, you may remember.'

'Yes.'

'The week previous to it I was invited to spend the evening with some people in the town who were kind to me, they having formerly lived near papa's rectory. Beauty was also invited out elsewhere the same evening. It chanced in returning home that we both reached the door together; an old maid-servant was my escort. Beauty's was a tall, handsome young man. She held his arm, and I divined, as by instinct, that her lover had come to Walborough. I had a good look at him; the gas-lamp shone right upon his face. He wished her good night abruptly, and was turning away when Agnes stopped him. "This is Miss Stanhope, of whom you have so often heard me speak," she said: and of course politeness compelled him to stop and say a few words to me. Not many: before the door was opened to us, he had lifted his hat, and was gone. "Don't tell of me, Susan," Beauty entreatingly whispered; "Miss Robertson might not like it."'

'And did you tell?'

'Why, of course not, Bessy. Would we tell tales of one another? Besides, there was no harm, that I saw, in his just walking home with her. I supposed the friends she had been with sanctioned it.'

'Go on.'

'The next week I left school, and entered on the situation Miss Robertson had procured for me at Lady Leslie's. It was a long, long way from Walborough; about midway, you know, between that place and this, Penryn; Beauty and I could not expect to meet often, but we promised each other, amid our farewell tears and kisses, to correspond constantly. Bessy, I never got but two letters from her.'

I felt surprised at Susan's tone more than at the words.

'But two letters. One of them was written from school; the other, only a week later, from London. She had left Walborough, she told me, and was staying with some friends in London until her marriage, which was to take place immediately, and she only wished I could go up to be her bridesmaid

—which of course was not to be thought of. After that, I never heard from her.'

'And have you never heard yet?'

'Listen. A few months later, at the close of August, I think, or beginning of September—I know it was a warm, hazy day—I was in the school-room, correcting exercises, my pupils being out walking with their French maid, when one of the servants came to say that a young lady was asking for me, and showed her in. It was Agnes: and, as the door closed, she fell into my arms with a sort of moan. How terribly the girl had changed in the five or six months since we parted I cannot express to you, Bessy; her once lovely face had become thin and drawn, her once pretty, rounded shoulders sharp. I could not speak for dismay; I saw something was wrong. She clung to me sobbing and shivering. "I was obliged to come to you on my journey, Susan, as this place lay in my way," she gasped out; "some power that I could not resist compelled me. It is only for a few minutes, Susan; only just to see you, Susan; and then I shall be gone again." "Are you married, dear Agnes?" I whispered, kissing her tenderly. "I *thought* I was, Susan," she said; "I thought it all that while, though he would not let me tell you, or anyone": and, with that, she sat down, poor weary girl, and laid her face, moaning, against the long desk. "You speak of a journey, dear," I said, "where are you going?" But she did not answer. There was a faint bluish tinge about her lips that I did not like; evidently she needed both food and rest. The thought came over me to beg of Lady Leslie to allow her to stay a day or two with me. I felt sure she would, being a kind, motherly woman. "Stay here a few moments, dear," I whispered, kissing her wan cheek. "I am going to bring you a glass of wine and a biscuit." Lady Leslie, I found, was with friends in the drawing-room; I hardly knew what to do, not liking to call her out, or to speak before them. While I was hesitating they came out to depart, and then I spoke to Lady Leslie, telling a little of Beauty's history, and hinting at my fears that something was wrong. "By all means, let Miss Garth stay for a few days," Lady Leslie warmly said; "if she is in distress or any kind of trouble, all the more need that her friends should see after her": the children might have holiday, and I could devote myself entirely to her. I was so pleased and grateful, Bessy, that I burst into tears. Then I ran to get a glass of wine from the butler, and returned to the school-room. It was empty. Beauty was gone.'

'Gone?'

'Quite gone. She must have left the school-room almost as soon as I: one of the servants met her in the hall and opened the door for her. Lady Leslie had enquiries made, and we found that Agnes had hastened back to the railway-station and taken the train onwards.'

'To London?'

'No, she had come from London. It was to Cornwall. There was some trouble about her ticket—a through ticket—because she had left the train. The railway clerk said it was made out for St Huth. Bessy, I have never seen or heard of her from that day to this.'

'St Huth is a small place about seven miles off beyond this.'

'I know. I traced it out upon the map and in "Bradshaw." But now—why do you suppose I have told you this story?'

Leaning forward to me as she put the question, I could not fail to see that Susan was agitated; her soft colour went and came; her beautiful blue eyes were strangely bright.

'That man, Hubert Arlegh, who is to marry Miss Bertram, over whose feet the white hare passed and repassed tonight, startling him to terror, was the lover of Agnes Garth.'

I uttered an exclamation of dismay.

'I knew him instantly, Bessy. Though I had seen him but once before, and then by gas-light. I recognized both himself and his voice, as he stood before me in the park lane tonight. It is a very peculiar voice: deep and gruff, as if it lay in his throat. You say Mr Arlegh's name is Hubert. *His* name was Hubert. Agnes never called him anything else. And what I want to know is this: if he is going to marry Miss Bertram, where is Agnes?'

I could not answer. Thought upon thought crowded my mind, each more unwelcome than the last. All in a moment, *another* thought—or, rather, a recollection—came up; and it was the worst of all.

'When do you say this was, Susan?—that she came into Cornwall?'

'Just about a year ago.'

Why yes, that was the very time. It was about a year ago now, so far as I could remember, that a young lady, weary.

anxious, footsore, found her way to the Widow Mellon's cottage. She lay ill there for two days, and then disappeared. They could not tell what became of her; nobody else could tell. Minnie Mellon told a curious tale—but, as people said, she was only a child. Nothing of this did I disclose to Susan, though the description of this young lady, given to me by Mrs Mellon's sister, who was then at the cottage, was exactly like the one Susan gave of Agnes Garth. It would not do for us Trenathys to bring up ought against Mr Arlegh. Once his marriage with Miss Bertram had taken place he would be our landlord to all intents and purposes—and my father would want his lease renewed the year after next.

We got to bed at last: but I could not speak for thinking of it all—of the story told by Susan, of Miss Bertram's ill-luck to be engaged to such a man, of the uncertain fate of poor Agnes Garth, and last, though not least, of the white hare that had run over Mr Arlegh's feet. I must have a spice of romance in my composition, I take it, for that white hare kept pushing itself into my thoughts above all the rest of the perplexity.

There had been some trouble lately with our poultry, especially the geese; many had sickened, and died; and in the morning, as soon as my various duties were over, I put on my sun-bonnet to run down to Michael Hart's, who was gamekeeper to Miss Bertram, to consult his wife, for she was learned in poultry. Mary Hart was not at home. However, Michael, smoking his after-dinner pipe at the cottage door, said she had stepped over towards the swamp-land, with a bit of stewed rabbit for old Widow Loam, who was ill—thought to be dying. I hardly knew whether to wait for Mary Hart or not; it was nearly one o'clock, our dinner-hour. Michael thought she would not be long; so down I sat upon the bench outside the kitchen-window and talked to him.

'Are there any white hares about, Michael?'

'White hares!' he exclaimed in his slow way, turning his head to look at me. 'Why no, Miss Bessy, we've no game o' that sort.'

'My cousin, Miss Stanhope, thought she saw a white hare cross the park lane yesterday evening.'

'Must ha' been a rabbit,' said Michael—just as I had said to Susan. 'Folks don't like the white hares in this country,' he added, changing his pipe from one hand to the other. 'They bode no good when seen.'

'But how can they be seen if there are none, Michael?'

'Well, it's thought they white hares are not real hares, but spirits, Miss Bessy; apparitions. I never saw a white hare but once, and don't want to see one again.'

'You have seen one, then?'

'I saw that one, Miss Bessy. It's a matter o' ten years ago. Do you remember as fur back as that?'

'Of course I do, Michael. I am twenty-two.'

'In that red house over yonder—you can see its chimbleys above the trees—lived old Trehern and his wife and son. Young Trehern was a bit wild, and gave 'em some trouble—but you'd know naught about that. One autumn day, when I was out with Sir William and a party and the guns and dogs, young Trehern, who made one o' the gentlemen, lagged behind the rest, telling me of a dog of his that had been sick; when, just as we were crossing the five-cornered coppice, a white hare—as it looked—ran out o' the brushwood right over his feet. Right over his feet, Miss Bessy; I never saw such a thing afore. Young Trehern didn't much like it; I could see that; and he jumped aside ever so far. He thought of the superstition, I suppose, but he made light of it to me. "What thing was that, Hart?" says he, swearing a bit and shaking his feet, as if he'd shake off the touch the thing had left on his boot. "It looked uncommon like a hare, sir," says I, "but 'twas gone so quick there's no telling." We went on then, and no more passed. Nine days after that young Trehern died. He was throwed out of his gig coming home from a dinner, and was killed on the spot.'

'And now, Michael, what is the superstition?'

Michael smoked for a full minute in his slow way before attempting to answer.

'It's not much the sort o' thing to tell to young ladies, Miss Bessy.'

'But I want to know it. I have a very particular reason for wishing to know it. I am a woman grown, remember, Michael; not a child.'

'Well, as to young Trehern, he had talked and laughed too much with Patty, the Widow Loam's daughter—her, by token, that Mary's gone to take the bit o' rabbit to—and then turned round and laughed at her for it. A pretty young thing she was; and 'twas told that the widow cursed him. I did not know how that might have been. Anyway, Patty died of it.'

'But the superstition, Michael?'

'That *is* the superstition, Miss Bessy. When a young girl gets treated in that way and dies of it, she comes back in the form of a white hare, whenever his own death shall be nigh at hand; comes back in love to give him warning of it.'

A slight shiver took me at the words. Could Mr Arlegh's death be near at hand? What a foolish thought! I mentally said, and threw off the shiver and superstition together. That we Cornish people hold to many ridiculous fancies I know, but surely not to one so ridiculous as this.

'Your wife does not seem to return, Michael,' I said, rising from the bench; 'so I will not wait longer. Perhaps she can come up to the farm; I should like her to see the geese.'

'She'll come safe enough, Miss Bessy.'

But, do what I would, I could not get these matters out of my mind. Not the superstition; that did not linger in it much; but the story Susan had told of Agnes Garth, and the curious likeness that seemed to exist between her and the girl who had gone to Mrs Mellon's, and the coincidence as regarded the time.

That afternoon we had tea unusually early, four o'clock, to accommodate my father, who was going out. I contrived to run down alone to Mrs Mellon's afterwards: I wanted to question her. Susan was busy over some strips of beautiful old pillow lace that had been her mother's, and which had got yellowish with lying by. It had been washed that afternoon and Susan was pulling it out preparatory to spreading it on the grass to bleach. It served as an excuse for my leaving her.

'What was the young lady like who came here about a year ago, Miss Bessy?' repeated Mrs Mellon, in answer to me. 'Well, you know, miss, I couldn't see her myself; but my sister Ann, who was over here just then, couldn't talk enough about her beauty and her wan looks and her dreadful sadness.'

'Very fair, was she not?—with blue eyes?'

'Oh very fair, and her eyes the bluest and sweetest and saddest, and her hair a bright golden colour. Minnie here was talking of her only last night, miss: she said that the young lady who came here from your house with the wool had just the same beautiful golden hair.'

It seemed to me like a confirmation, and I drew a long

breath. 'Will you tell me the particulars of her coming, and of her stay here?' I asked.

'It is a matter of a year ago, Miss Bessy. We were having our tea at this round table one afternoon, Ann, and me, and the child, when we heard a sort of stir outside, and Ann went to the door. There stood at it a young girl dressed in black, pale and weary, as if she had travelled far, with a wan, lovely face. Would we allow her to sit down for a few minutes, she asked, and give her a drink of water, for she felt faint. Ann brought her in, and she fainted right off in the chair as she sat down. Well, Miss Bessy, we undressed her and put her into Minnie's bed, for she was a great deal too ill and weak to go away that night. And in that bed she stayed nigh upon three days, not strong enough to get out of it, and crying a'most all the time, and—'

'Did she tell you her name?' I interrupted.

'She never told her name, nor where she belonged to, nor anything else about herself. But she did say she had walked over from St Huth early that morning. We thought she must have been waiting about here all the day since, as if waiting for somebody, for two or three people saw her; and Michael Hart he said—but he told me afterwards I had better not speak of that,' broke off Mrs Mellon, 'so I'll let it alone. On the third day she got up, Miss Bessy, and I remember well as she sat here with me after our bit of dinner—Ann was gone—she asked me many questions about Miss Bertram and the marriage it was said she was going to make with Mr Arlegh—just as if she had knowed Miss Rosy afore. Leastways it struck me so, and I put the question to her plain. No, she had never seen Miss Bertram in her life, she answered, but she had heard of her. After that, I heard her stirring about, and it seemed that she was putting her bonnet and mantle on to leave. I asked her whether she was sure she was strong enough, and whether she had far to go. "Not far, only a little way," she answered me, and she felt quite strong. With that, she took off a locket that she had worn on her neck, fastened to some blue ribbon, and put it upon Minnie's neck. "Keep it, my dear," she said to her; "it is all I have to give you, and I shall not want it where I am going." Upon that she wished me goodbye very hastily, and was gone from the door afore I could say a word, leaving (as I found afterwards) a gold sovereign wrapped in a bit o' paper on the table at my elbow.

"Run, Minnie," I says, "and see which way she goes, and watch her a bit," for I thought it likely she might faint again, besides feeling anxious about her. So Minnie ran, and watched her ever so far—down to the swamp-land, wasn't it child?'

'Yes, mother,' replied Minnie, an elfish-looking child of ten, who had been listening with both her ears. 'I kept behind her all the way, watching her till I couldn't see her no longer. She went down the lane to the swamp-land, and she never came out again.'

'Never came out again,' I exclaimed, the phrase striking me as an odd one. 'How do you mean, Minnie?'

'She never did come out,' replied Minnie. 'I stood watching for her ever so long.'

'The child means that she never saw her come out,' put in the mother. 'She didn't like to follow her too close, for fear of being seen.'

'Did you follow her down the lane, Minnie?'

'After a bit I did. I saw her under they willows that edges the swamp on this side, and I stopped by the trees half way down the lane to see where she went to. When I didn't see her come back nor nothing, I went on to they willows too, but she was gone.'

'But where could she go to?' I cried, something like a panic seizing my heart. 'She could not walk over the swamp to gain the road: she would sink into it.'

'I'm sure she never came back down the lane,' repeated Minnie. 'I never see her come.'

'She must have managed to get round the swamp by they dwarf stumps o' trees, Miss Bessy, and so gained the high road that way,' put in Mrs Mellon, her quiet, matter-of-fact tone proving that no worse thought had ever occurred to her.

'You do not think she could have—have got *into* the swamp?' I asked, scarcely above my breath.

The woman turned her sightless face to me in surprise. Minnie stared with wondering eyes. The idea to them seemed very far-fetched.

'Why no, Miss Bessy, there was no fear o' that kind. There wouldn't be. Had the poor young lady lost her footing and fell in, which was not likely, she'd naturally ha' cried out; and there was Minnie at hand to hear her.'

The conviction that, had she put herself in purposely she would *not* have cried out, ran through my mind like a flash of lightning: and then I mentally called myself a wicked girl for thinking it. 'Would you let me see the locket she gave Minnie?' I asked aloud.

Dame Mellon took a small key from her pocket, felt her way to the dresser, and unlocked a tea-caddy that stood on it. 'I keep it locked up for fear Minnie should lose it,' she remarked, placing it in my hands; 'they small things is so easy dropped, and children be so careless.'

Ah! no need to take a second look. The golden locket had a lock of golden hair inside it—Susan's hair beyond all doubt—and it bore the inscription 'Susan to Agnes.'

'I should like to show this to my cousin: it is very pretty,' I said impulsively. 'Will you let me take it home, Mrs Mellon? You shall have it back tomorrow.'

Ready permission was given, and I was desired not to be in a hurry to return the locket. The old woman took her stick, and walked with me, talking, to the little bridge. Some children were playing at the entrance to the park lane, and Minnie ran off to them.

'I wish you would tell me one thing,' I said in a low tone—'what it was that Michael Hart told you. You may trust me, you know.'

'Dear, yes, I may, Miss Bessy. Well, Michael saw the young lady that same afternoon, talking with Mr Arlegh in the coppice. He was coming home from shooting, and she darted out from the coppice, as if she had put herself there to wait for him, and laid her hand upon his arm. Mr Arlegh shook her hand off, and swore at her; asking where she had sprung from, and what she wanted: Michael heard that much, as he walked onwards with the dogs. Half an hour later he came by again and they were there still. She was crying and moaning bitterly; and he was calling her a tramp, in harsh tones, and threatening to give her into custody for molesting him, unless she went back at once to "whence she came." Michael didn't know how the quarrel ended; except that Mr Arlegh must have left her there, for he presently saw him cross the park lane on his way to the Hall. It wasn't a thing to talk about, you see, Miss Bessy, and that's why he wanted me to be silent.'

All sorts of troubles were worrying my brain as I went home. It was poor Agnes Garth safe enough. But what could I do in it? And where was she?

Very much to my surprise, when I came within sight of our

gate, I saw Mr Arlegh's horse fastened to it, and himself on the grassplat with Susan. She had her hands folded before her, and her face, as she spoke to him, wore a cold, haughty expression. Suddenly he wheeled round on his heel, came out, mounted his horse and rode past me, not vouchsafing me any notice by word or look. Susan explained to me what had happened.

She was spreading her lace on the grass, putting a stone at the ends of each piece to secure it, when Mr Arlegh rode by. Seeing Susan, he checked his horse suddenly, dismounted, and came in.

'So you are one of Farmer Trenathy's daughters, my dear,' he began, in a free tone that Susan did not like at all. 'And where have you been hiding yourself pray, that I never saw you before last night?'

'Mr Trenathy is my uncle,' replied Susan, turning from the lace to face him.

'Have you come to live here?'

'No.'

'To stay for a time, at any rate, I conclude. I am very glad. It is not often we get such beauty as yours in this out-of-the-world place.'

'Mr Arlegh,' began Susan, 'you have taken upon yourself to ask me questions. In return, may I put one or two to you?'

'Fifty if you like, my dear. The more the better.'

'When you were quite a lad, were you not placed for three or four years with the Reverend Philip Stanhope, of Grassmere? That lad's name was, I know, Hubert Arlegh.'

'Just so. Mr Stanhope was my tutor.'

'You respected and liked him, I believe.'

'Liked and respected Stanhope! I just did. What next?'

'I am his daughter—Miss Stanhope—and a gentlewoman, Mr Arlegh.'

He seemed quite taken to, and his face flushed, Susan said. But he had the grace to change his manner to one of respect, offered his hand, and said he was glad to see her.

'There is another question I wish to ask you, and it is a painful one,' Susan went on; 'one very painful to me to put. Can you tell me where Agnes Garth is?'

He stared at her for a moment, his countenance visibly changing. 'Agnes Garth!' he presently rejoined, breaking the silence. 'I do not know any one of the name.'

'I think you did know her, Mr Arlegh. She was my best friend, dear to me as a sister: we were at school together at Walborough. For this past twelve month I have been anxiously waiting for news from her, watching for it daily: and it never comes.'

'I protest I cannot understand why you should say this to me, Miss Stanhope,' he replied, his manner cold, his tone repellant. 'I never heard of the person you mention. Allow me to wish you good evening.' And, with that, he turned quickly, as I had seen him turn, and took his departure.

Susan told me this as we sat side by side on the bench under the large pear-tree, the horse's hoofs dying away in our ears as they grew more distant. I held out the gold locket on my glove.

'Do you know this, Susan?'

She caught hold of it, gave one look, and burst into tears. 'Oh Bessy, where did you get this? It was the keepsake I gave to Agnes when I left school. She gave me that pretty cross that I wear, in exchange.'

I told her all—even my doubts and fears about the swamp. It is true I had not meant to say so much: but tales, at such moments, expand in the telling. 'But, Susan dear,' I added, in conclusion, 'you must keep all this strictly quiet. It would not do to stir in it for my father's sake.'

'*I* keep it quiet!' she retorted, turning her tearful eyes upon me. 'Why, Bessy, do you imagine this is a thing we mortals can control? If my poor Agnes does indeed lie in that swamp-land, rely upon it that a Higher Power holds its elucidation in His hands.'

The stars were beginning to twinkle in the sky, the moon was rising, the scent of the closing flowers was almost lost on the cool air; and still we sat on. Out came Eunice, wondering why we stayed there when we must know the early supper was ready.

'You will take me to look at this swamp-land tomorrow, Bessy,' whispered Susan, as we rose. 'I cannot rest until I see it.' And I promised.

But, like many another promise, it was not fated to be performed. Some friends, not expected, came over from St Huth in the morning to spend the day with us, and the next day it was raining, pouring cats and dogs—as Janey said when she had to go through it to school; aye, and the next day also. Altogether, the following week had come in when we went.

The sun, glowing and red, and nearing its setting, was shining on this marsh land as we gazed upon it. It was a curious looking spot—half water, half earth, wholly black mud—as it seemed to Susan. In Sir William's time he would not have had this bay touched—it would be valuable sometime, he said, but *he* should not trouble himself to make it so. It lay about as far from our house, on that side, as the Hall did on the other. The willows, spoken of by Mrs Mellon, drooped over the edge of a portion of it, then came a crowd of rushes, then the dwarf trees, some of them only stumps.

'You see, Susan,' I observed, 'she could have crept round by the rushes and stumps, and so gained the road.'

'Yes, I see,' replied Susan; 'it would have been possible, I suppose. On the other hand, she may have thrown herself in, to escape her troubled life.'

'*Don't* think it, Susan, for heaven's sake!'

As we regained the road, which was narrow just there, not much better, indeed, than a lane, Miss Bertram drove up in her pretty low carriage, drawn by its cream-coloured pony, Mr Arlegh sitting beside her. She pulled up to speak to me, and he raised his hat.

Suddenly, as if it sprang out of the ground, for I'm sure I saw not where else it could have come from, a white hare was disporting itself under the pony's feet. Whether it was a real hare or a phantom, the pony became curiously terrified, his eyes glaring, his mouth foaming. The hare disappeared almost instantly, but the animal continued to rear and plunge. Miss Bertram was a remarkably timid girl, although she did drive this hitherto quiet pony: she dropped the reins, and would have leaped out. Mr Arlegh prevented her, jumped out himself, and went to the pony's head. He had not, I am sure, seen the hare.

But he saw now. The hare—and this seemed to me the strangest part of it—the hare, which had certainly disappeared, was back again, running over *his* feet. With a sort of suppressed yell, Mr Arlegh jumped back and loosed his hold of the pony. Again the hare had disappeared; he re-caught the pony's head, and Miss Bertram jumped out.

'Selim, what can be the matter with you?' she cried, addressing the pretty and trembling cream-coloured animal. 'Did you see anything frighten him?' she added to me. 'Did you, Hubert?'

But what could I answer? Nothing. Mr Arlegh was now leading the pony forward, and when he seemed quiet, they got in and drove off, Mr Arlegh taking the reins.

Once more, but this time we only knew of it by hearsay, Mr Arlegh was frightened by the white hare. It was on the following Sunday. He was walking across the churchyard with our clergyman, Mr Chasnel, they having stayed in the vestry after service to discuss some parish business, when, just as they were going by old Mrs Barton's high tomb, a white hare ran across Mr Arlegh's feet; seemed to *stand* on them for a moment.

'Why that looked just like a hare!' cried the clergyman. 'Where's it gone to? Has it startled you?' he added to Mr Arlegh, seeing that his face had turned whiter than death.

'I—don't know what it was,' replied Mr Arlegh, as they looked about. But the hare was gone.

The Reverend Charles Chasnel talked of this—that's how it came to be known. He told people that he had seen a white hare. Being a stranger in Cornwall, just appointed to the living, he had never heard of the superstition.

'What news do you think I have got?' cried Roger, coming in to breakfast on the Tuesday morning. 'That old bog is going to be redeemed. Drained, and—'

'I'll believe it when I see it,' interrupted father. 'Sir William was always talking of that, but he never did it, and the fields around are nothing but a marsh. It has long been the shame of the place.'

'It is really going to be done now,' said Roger, smiling at his father's vehemence. 'Some gentlemen are coming to the Hall today about it; scientific men from London; and the work is to be begun immediately. The bailiff himself told me. They say,' and here Roger laughed outright, 'that there's great value in that swamp, as it now is.'

Father looked at him quite angrily. '*Value* in it?'

'In the mud—or the water—or both combined. They talk of its chemical properties. It is Mr Arlegh who has set all this in motion, Stone says, and has persuaded Miss Bertram to have it done.'

'Time it was,' grunted father. That swamp had always been a sore point with him.

WAS IT 'THE FLYING DUTCHMAN'?

Years long ago, one night, a gig's crew was called to go off to a 'hobble', to the westwards of St Ives Head. No sooner was one boat launched than several others were put off from the shore, and a stiff chase was maintained, each one being eager to get to the ship, as she had the appearance of a foreign trader. The hull was clearly visible, she was a schooner-rigged vessel, with a light over her bows.

Away they pulled, and the boat which had been first launched still kept ahead by dint of mechanical power and skill. All the men had thrown off their jackets to row with more freedom. At length the helmsman cried out, 'Stand ready to board her.' The sailor rowing the bow oar slipped it out of the row-lock, and stood on the forethought, taking his jacket on his arm, ready to spring aboard.

The vessel came so close to the boat that they could see the men, and the bow-oar man made a grasp at her bulwarks. His hand found nothing solid, and he fell, being caught by one of his mates, back into the boat, instead of into the water. Then ship and lights disappeared. The next morning the *Neptune* of London, Captain Richard Grant, was wrecked at Gwithian, and all perished. The captain's body was picked up after a few days, and that of his son also. They were both buried in Gwithian churchyard.

ROBERT HUNT

THE IRON PINEAPPLE

EDEN PHILLPOTTS

It will comfort me to write it. It comforted me to tell my wife, but that consolation vanished when she refused to believe the story and proposed to send for a medical man.

There may be scientific people who could explain what happened to me; there may be names for the state, and it is possible that others have suffered similarly, and done equally amazing things, but in my humble position of life one has no time for works on morbid psychology or its therapeutics, and I prefer to explain all differently and directly. I choose rather to assert that it pleased Providence to select me on a unique occasion for its own profound purposes.

That is how I explain it now, but to be the weapon of Providence in a great matter is not a part that any sane small shopkeeper would choose, and none will ever know the extent of my sufferings while the secret forces that control our destinies had their terrible way with me; none will ever fathom my awful woes and fears as I tottered on the brink of downright madness; none will ever look into the unutterable chasm that for a season yawned between me and my fellow-creatures.

I was cut off from them; I lived a hideous life apart. No human eyes penetrated those dark fastnesses of the spirit where I wandered, lost; no friendly voice sounded for me; no sympathy nor understanding came to my side and heartened me to conquer the appalling tribulation.

Doubtless, in some measure, the fault was my own. There were not a few who respected me, and would have done all they might to help me. My wife—what man ever had better? She was always ready, and her gentle tact paved a way for me through many a neurotic storm and morbid ecstasy, but the secret thing, the obsession of my life, was hidden from her. For shame I hid it; even to her I could not confess its nature and the profound and shattering effect it had upon my self-control and my self-respect.

The nature of this curse will best appear in the course of my narrative. John Noy is my name, and I dwell in the Cornish haven of Bude. Hither from Holsworthy I came, twenty years ago, but the prosperity that has of late burst in a grateful shower over Bude, converting it from an obscure hamlet to a prosperous resort, was not shared by me.

I keep a small grocery-store, and sell fruit and vegetables also; while to eke out my modest means I control a branch of the post-office, and so add little to my income, but much to my daily labours; for the paltry remuneration of one pound one shilling a month is all that accrues to me for my service in this great department of the State.

I had hoped that in the rising districts of Flexbury, where new houses were springing up like mushrooms, and often with little more than a mushroom's stability, the post-office might have opened a way to increased custom, and added to the importance and popularity of my little business. But it never did so. Occasional notepaper and sealing-wax I disposed of, but no respectable augmentation of my own trade could be chronicled as a result of the post-office, while, in holiday time, the work proved—and still proves—too much for one head and one pair of hands. Then my clever wife comes to my assistance; and, even so, our accounts do not alway balance.

Of course, Bude is not what it was when first I wedded Mabel Polglaze and took my shop. Now an enormous summer population pours upon us annually, and the golf-links swarm with men and women, who pursue that sport from dawn till evening; and the wide sands of the shore are covered with children who, in their picturesque attire, are scattered there, like pink and blue, yellow and white flower-petals blowing over the sands when the tide is out.

I never had any children; and it was a grief to my wife, but a secret joy to me—not because I do not love them, but because, after marriage, my infatuation dawned upon me, and I quickly felt that to hand on such mysterious traits of character would be criminal in the opinion of any conscientious soul.

The cloud ascended by slow degrees upon my clear horizon, and not until it had assumed some quality of sinister significance did I give it much thought. Indeed, in its earliest manifestation, I took pride in it; and my wife, even from our betrothal, was wont to compliment me upon a certain quality of mind often associated with ultimate prosperity and worldly success.

'Noy,' she said to me on one occasion, 'your grasp of details is the most remarkable thing about you. You'll fasten on a thing, like a dog on a bone, and nought will shake you off it. Whether 'tis sardines, or dried fruits, or spring vegetables, or a new tea, 'twill grip your mind in a most amazing way, and you'll let everything else slip by, and just go for that one object, and keep it in the front of your thoughts, and live on it, like food. And a very fine quality in a grocer; and many a time you've pushed a line and made the public take a new thing. But what's queer about it, in my judgment, is that, so often as not, you'll put all your heart and soul into some stupid little matter, like a new mouse-trap or new vermin-killer, that don't pay for the trouble. You'll give just so much thought to a penwiper or bottle-washer, not worth sixpence, as you will to a new drink or new food, or some big thing that might mean good money, and plenty of it.'

There she hit the nail on the head. I had a way to take some particular matter into my mind, as the hedge-sparrow takes the cuckoo's egg into her nest, and then, when the thing hatched out, all else had to go down before it, and for a season I was a man of one idea, and only one. Had those ideas been important; had I conceived brilliant plans for Bude, or even for myself, none could have quarrelled with this power of concentration, or suspected that any infirmity of mind lurked behind it, but, as my wife too faithfully pointed out, I was prone to expend my rich stores of nervous energy upon the most trifling and insignificant matters.

Once I caught a grasshopper in our little garden, and for two years I had no mind to anything but grasshoppers. I purchased works on entomology which I could ill afford; I collected grasshoppers, and spent long hours in studying their manners and customs; I tamed a grasshopper, and finally acquired a knowledge of these insects that has probably never been equalled in the history of the world.

I fought this down with my wife's help, but it was the beginning of worse things; and after she had lost her temper, and expressed her opinion of such puerilities in good set terms, I grew afraid, and began to conceal my mind from her. Then I found that, unconsciously, my frankness in all matters of the soul with Mabel had helped to keep me straight, and been a shield between me and the horrid idiosyncrasies of my nature.

The descent to hell was easy, and, after barriers were once raised between my aberration and her common sense, the former grew by leaps and bounds. A change came over my horrid interests. Formerly it was some comestible or contrivance in my shop that had fixed my attention and chained my energies, to the loss of more important things; for the grasshoppers arrived, as it were, before their time, and for many years after I had struggled free of their influence I suffered no similar lapse. But, having once adopted the practice of simulation with Mabel, having once withheld from her the secrets of my heart, the deterioration proceeded apace: I ceased to be vitally interested in my shop; I wandered afield, and fastened on subjects and objects altogether outside my own life. These I brought into the very heart of my own mystery, and welcomed and worshipped. They were unconceivably trivial: in that lay the growing horror.

To give an example: I remembered how for a time one monument in the churchyard arrested and absorbed my receptive faculties. Many nameless dead, victims of the sea, sleep their last sleep in our green churchyard upon the hill, and here, above a ship's company drowned long since at the haven mouth, there stands with a certain propriety the figure-head of their wrecked vessel. As it advanced before them in life, hanging above the ocean and leaping to the wave, so now in death the image keeps guard above their pillows, and stands, tall and white, among the lesser monuments of the mortuary. So it has stood for nearly fifty years, and promises long to continue, for it is preserved carefully and guarded against destruction.

This wooden image of the ill-fated *Bencoolan* exercised a most dreadful fascination over me; and I cannot tell now how often I visited it, touched it, and poured out my futile thoughts as an offering to it. The figure of the Asiatic chieftain became to me an incubus and exercised a mesmeric power of attraction under which for a season I suffered helplessly. Indeed, I only escaped by abandoning the Church of England and joining the sect of the Primitive Wesleyans. I avoided the church and the grave of the drowned men; I struggled against the horrible attraction of the figure-head. At night I woke and sweated and fought to keep in my couch, and I locked my arms through the bedstead that I might not be torn away to that solemn effigy above the graves.

The Primitive Wesleyans had a chapel within ten minutes' walk of my shop. It was new; the foundation-stone had been laid but two years before by that famous Wesleyan philanthropist, financier and friend of man, Bolsover Barbellion. The building, in the last and most debased form of architecture ever sprung from a mean mind, dominated Flexbury, and stood, a mass of hideous stone and baleful brick, above the pitiful rows of new dwelling-houses. But it saved me from the figure-head of the *Bencoolan*, and for a time the ministrations of the Primitive Wesleyans soothed my soul, and offered peace through the channels of religious novelty. I owe them much, and gladly record my debt.

Instances as grim as the foregoing might be cited, but I hasten to the climax of the tragedy and the events that preceded it. My wife, after a lengthened period, during which too surely we had drifted apart in sympathy and mutual understanding, took me to task, and her acerbity, while well enough deserved, none the less caused me a wide measure of astonishment. Never had she struck this note until this hour.

'Why the mischief can't you turn your attention to keeping a roof over our heads?' she asked. 'Trade's never been worse, and you'll lose the post-office afore another summer if you make any more mistakes. And here's things happening in the world that might make angels weep. Look at yesterday's paper—all of them benevolent societies come down like a pack of cards, and that saint of God, as we thought—that Bolsover Barbellion—turns out to be a limb of Satan instead. And your own sister ruined, and widows and orphans face to face with the workhouse from one end of England to the other! And the scoundrel himself has vanished like the dew upon the fleece, as well he may do. And there's another coal strike, the like of which was never knowed, and there's a murder to Plymouth, and talk of war with Germany, and God knows what beside! Yet you—you can live in this world as if you was no more than a sheep or a cow, and pour out your wits in secret on some twopenny-halfpenny thing that you be too ashamed even to speak about. Yes; you can, and you do. I know you—if not me, who should? I hear you a-tossing like a ship in a storm of a night, and you won't let me comfort you no more. And life's hell to a woman placed like me, and I don't say how much longer I'm going to stand it! How do I know what's in your mind? How can I help you and comfort you if I'm kept outside in the dark? All I can tell is that you're mad on something, for you're always out now—always walking up and down on the cliffs as if you was a sentry or a coastguard. And some fine day you'll fall over, and that'll be a nice scandal; for there's no smoke without fire, and of course they'll whisper 'twas me that drove you to it.'

Thus she ran on, and I made no attempt to stay the torrent. My last infatuation differed widely from all others, for it was human; and had it been a woman, by evil chance, doubtless my home had crashed down under it, for Mrs Noy was not of the type that tolerates any largeness of view in matters of sex. But a man had for three months exercised an unconscious control upon me—a large, bearded, able-bodied artist, who devoted his attention to our cliff scenery, and who painted pictures in the open air on Bude sands.

I never spoke to him. He was not even aware that he had an interested spectator, but from the day I first looked over the low cliffs near the cricket-ground, and saw the top of the painter's hat, I was lost, and became concentrated upon the man. He dominated my thoughts, and I felt ill at ease on the days that I did not see him. I made no effort to learn his name or ascertain where he lodged, but I speculated deeply concerning him and the value of his art, and the workings of his mind and his ambitions and hopes and fears. He had an interesting face and a large voice, and rejoiced to watch the children playing on the beach. He painted ill—so, at least, I thought.

It seemed to me that he was an impressionist, and I felt aversion from that school, being ignorant of its principles. Once he left his seat among the rocks to walk beside the sea a while, and I emerged from the cliff above, whence I had been watching him, and descended and looked at his picture. Something urged me to sit on his camp-stool, and I did so. He turned, saw me, and approached. But the tide was out, and he had to walk nearly a quarter of a mile to his easel. I hastened away and hid from him, and watched him exhibit no small surprise when he returned. He examined his picture closely to see that I had not meddled with it.

From that day I conceived a violent dislike to the artist, and this emotion increased to loathing; then waxed from that until it grew into an acute and homicidal hatred. Why such an awful passion should have wakened in me against this harmless painter it was impossible to understand.

I had never hated man or mouse until that moment; and now, full-fledged, insistent, tigerish, there awoke within me an antagonism one would have supposed impossible to so mild a mannered man. I fought it as I had never fought any previous obsession; I told myself that rather than do any violence to a fellow-creature I would destroy my own body. Time and again, tramping the cliffs to peep down upon the unconscious painter beneath, I urged myself to take a false step, and do even as my wife had predicted that I might do. To escape from this fiendish premonition, to die and be at peace, grew an ever-increasing temptation. But I lacked physical courage; I could not kill myself. I would have endured any mental torment rather than do so.

I met the painter face to face sometimes, and a demon might have felt his anti-human passion grow weak before the man's kind, good-natured face, great brown beard, laughing brown eyes, and sonorous, genial voice, but my antipathy only increased. It was, so far as I could analyse, quite without motive—a mere destructive instinct that made me tremble to batter and crush out of living this fellow-soul.

I determined to consult a medical man, but hesitated to do so for fear that he would insist upon my incarceration. I was not mad—save in the particular of my passing infatuations; and, as all the others until now had persisted only for a season, I wept on my knees and prayed to Heaven through long night watches that this awful and crowning trial might also pass from me, and give place to hallucinations less terrific and less fraught with peril to my fellow-creatures.

As if in answer to this prayer there came sudden and astounding relief; my aberrations changed their direction; for a season I forgot the painter as though he had never been born, and every hope, desire, and mental energy became concentrated on the humblest and most insignificant object it is possible to mention. It was the lowest depth that I had reached.

On rising ground, not far distant from my shop, were being erected certain new dwelling-houses, and one of these had always pleased me, because it stood as an oasis in the dreary desert of mean buildings rising round about. It was designed in the Italian style, and possessed a distinction, beauty and reserve foreign to the neighbourhood of Bude and the architectural spirit of the district. An outer wall encompassed this dwelling, and light metalwork ran along the top of it.

To my horror I discovered that a conventional chain was to be erected, and, at intervals of ten feet, the chain was supported by metal pillars crowned with cast-iron pineapples. Why a pleasing building should thus be spoiled by a piece of gratuitous vulgarity I could not understand. But speculation swiftly ceased, for suddenly, like a bolt from the blue, as such ebullitions always came, there burst upon me a frantic lust for one of these same abortions in iron! My soul poured out upon a metal pineapple; and no general hunger or distributed desire for the vile things took hold of me, but I found my life's energy focused and concentrated upon the third pineapple on the north side of the railing. For the rest I entertained no attachment; I even disliked them; but the third on the northern side exercised an absolute mastery.

If one may quote a familiar jest in connection with so abhorrent a circumstance, I felt, concerning this hideous piece of cast-iron, that I should not be happy until I got it. Naked roads stretched about this new house. They ran through fields, presently to be built upon, and they were usually deserted, as they led no whither. I was able, therefore, to haunt the iron pineapple, to stroke it, gloat over it, and gratify in some sort my abnormal desire towards it without exciting attention. Indeed, the cunning of actual lunacy marked each new downfall, and, with the exception of Mabel, no human creature as yet had suspected my infirmity.

The pineapple swiftly became an all-absorbing passion, and I fought against its fascination without avail. The desire for possession made this experience especially difficult, because as a rule the attractive object always drew me to be with it, whereas, in this case, there came a frantic longing to have the pineapple with me. I must have thought of the rubbish as a sentient being; I must have exaggerated it into a creature that could feel and sorrow and understand. On wet nights I conceived that the iron pineapple might suffer cold; on hot days I feared that it was enduring discomfort from the summer sun! From the ease and peace of my bed, I pictured the pineapple perched on its lonely pedestal in outer darkness. When there raged a thunderstorm, I feared that the lightning would strike the pineapple and destroy it for ever.

Then an overwhelming determination to secure the pineapple quite possessed me. Therefore I stole it by night. At an hour when a waning moon silvered that rising district of empty houses and unbounded roads, I set forth, crept into the shadow of the Italian dwelling, and after working with a file for half an hour, won the valueless treasure. Once, during my operations, a policeman passed upon his beat; and I hid in the porch hard by and wondered what the man would have done had he discovered the post-master and provision merchant, John Noy, thus occupied between the morning hours of two and three.

To a sleeping wife I returned, and the pineapple was concealed in a drawer that contained my Sunday clothes.

The mass of metal weighed two pounds, and for a week I racked my brains to find fresh hiding-places for it. Now I concealed it under the earth in my garden; now I hid it in the shop; now I took it about with me, wrapped in a parcel.

The trash was never out of my mind. Moreover, a reward of one guinea had been offered for discovery of the person responsible for its disappearance. The owner of the Italian villa himself brought a printed advertisement to me containing the promise. I stuck it up against my shop-window with two blue wafers, and soothed him. He was much annoyed, and declared that a fool capable of such wilful and aimless destruction should be captured and locked up for the benefit of the community. How cordially I agreed with him! And all the while I looked down at a sack of dried peas at his feet, in which the iron pineapple was hidden.

And now the psychology of the mental situation took a turn, and my last two phases of infatuation ran into each other, as one line of rails merges into the next. The iron pineapple and the artist were inextricably mingled in my distracted mind. The one I loved, the other I hated; and I told myself that not until these two concrete ideas had come together and completed their diverse destinies might my own soul hope for any sort of peace.

So Providence set my brain to the task of fulfilling its inscrutable designs while I, ignorant of that supernatural purpose, merely looked into the darkness of my own heart and cowered before the lurid phantom of madness that I seemed to see advancing upon me from within it. I believed myself now definitely insane, but I was powerless to save the situation; indeed, an instinct far stronger than that of self-preservation held me in absolute subjection.

I walked on the cliffs and in the lonely lanes, and babbled my problem to the seagulls and the wayside flowers. By night

I submitted it to the stars of heaven. In sleep I uttered it aloud, as my wife testified too surely on an occasion of my waking.

We slept with a night-lamp, and on suddenly returning to consciousness I perceived Mabel sitting up and regarding my prostrate form in dismay. The extremity of concern marked her features. I recollect how the shadow of her head (decorated with curling-pins, or some other metal contrivances which hung from it, glittering in the mild beam of the night-light) was thrown enormous upon the ceiling, in an outline that suggested the map of the continent of Africa.

'Holy angels!' she began. 'What's the matter with you now? You've been babbling like something out of a child's fairy book—like that there *Alice in Wonderland* Mrs Hussey lent you, and you thought was funny, and I couldn't for the life of me laugh over. You keep on: "The pineapple and the painter; the painter and the pineapple, and quantities of sand!" And if I'm going mad, you'd better tell me so; and if I'm not, then, sure as quarter-day, you are. It can't go on. No woman could stand it!'

I strove to lead her mind into other channels. I explained that I wanted my signboard repainted, and that I proposed to buy a few West Indian pines from time to time to add to the attractions of our fruit department. We then discussed the advent of my only sister—an elderly spinster ruined by the recent collapse of certain benevolent societies. Between a home under my roof and the union workhouse there was literally no choice for her, and, ill as I could afford to support her, my sense of duty left me no alternative but to do so.

It fell out, however, that the forthcoming day was to witness greater matters than the arrival of Susan Noy at Bude. Of late the terrific problem of how to bring the loved pineapple and the hated painter together had made me more than usually inattentive to business. I wandered much, and chiefly by the sea it was that I passed my time. At low tide I walked upon the sands, or sat and brooded among the gaunt rocks, where purple mussels grew in clusters like grapes. At high tide I tramped the cliffs, and reclining upon them, watched the ships pass by on the horizon of the ocean; or gazed where Lundy, like a blue cloud, arose from the waves.

Here I was in the company of elemental things, and from them alone at this season did my tortured spirit win any sort of hope. The breaking billows and the broad pathway of light that fell upon them at sunset; the dark faces of the rocks, that watched from under beetling brows for the coming storm; the passage of wine-coloured shadows on the sea; the anthem of the great west wind, that made the precipice his cymbal and the crag his harp—these things alone brought a measure of peace to my soul. But calm it wholly they could not; solve the grotesque problem, that haunted me like a presence, they could not. I lived only to know how the iron pineapple and the cliff painter should be brought together into one idea—indivisible, corporate, compact.

It was fitting that the problem of a lunatic should be solved by a madman. For mad I most certainly was upon this day—one of God's chosen, to work His will through the dark machinery of a temporary mental alienation, a man deliberately robbed of his reason through certain terrific moments that the Everlasting Will might be manifested upon earth to the vindication of His all-watchfulness and justice!

The hour was after noon, the day one in late August, and I walked out upon the cliffs at a moment when general exodus from shore began; for the luncheon-time approached, and a long line of children, mothers, and nursemaids began to drift away inland from the pleasures of the beach. At one o'clock cliffs and shore were alike deserted for a season, and a pedestrian might also cross the links with safety. The golfers had ceased from troubling.

Now, upon a high cliff north of the bathing-places I wandered, weighted literally, as well as mentally, by my eternal problem. For in my breast-pocket, bulging and dragging me forward at a more acute angle than usual, was the iron pineapple. Why, I know not. But often now I carried it with me, and, when hidden from gaze of man, would display it as though study of the actual object was likely to help my deliberations.

Today, at the cliff-edge, I dragged it out, and laid it down where the short turf was already becoming seared under August suns. A dwarf betony, with purple bloom, grew at my elbow, and cushions of pink thrift, their blossoms now reduced to mere empty, silver tufts, clung close at hand on the cliff-faces. One crow's-feather, fallen on the grass, moved two yards away as the wind touched it, and the sun flashed upon its shining black plume; upon the downs a red sheep or two browsed on the sweet, close herbage. Inland rose the low hills, with their stunted trees and grey church towers ascending above them.

I was as lonely as man might be. The world had been deserted that our holiday folk might eat; and I realised to the full at this moment how entirely had Bude become a pleasure-resort, how absolutely it depended for prosperity upon those who, when their hours of respite came, hastened to North Cornwall for change of air and a place to play in. Not until the eye passed far south to the breakwater and lock and little canal running therefrom, not until it marked the ketches lying there, did one perceive any human enterprises other than those devoted to amusement and relaxation.

The iron pineapple stood upon the turf at my hand. The lump of iron was polished to brightness by constant handling, and it flashed back the sunshine from the planes of the cone.

For a long time I stared at it, and revolved my fatuous problem. Then suddenly, from far below on the beach, there arose the sound of a human voice singing a song. It was a mellow, juicy voice; it was a mellow, juicy song. The first I recognised quickly enough; the second I had never heard before. To this day I cannot say whence came the words or tune, but they served well enough to express the singer's present contentment.

To sing such a pæan of joy with such infinite relish and abandonment proved beyond possibility of doubt that the lonely creature below me was happy, hopeful, and contented with his life and its possibilities. 'He must,' said I, 'have sold one of his strange pictures at a good profit to himself, or he must have chanced on a kindred spirit, and met a heart that beats with his, an eye that sees with him. Life for him has surely brought some fresh beauty or joy, interest or fair promise, else he could not thus warble from his very soul with such bird-like content!' Needless to add that it was my big, brown-bearded artist who sang while he painted below.

I crept on my breast to the stark edge of the cliff, and looked down at him. He sat immediately beneath me, and I had leisure to note the curious perspective of his figure thus seen from high above his head. He wore a great grey wide-awake, and, beneath it, strangely foreshortened, bulged his big body squatted on a camp-stool. His legs did not appear; they were tucked under him. But his arms were visible. One hand held a palette and brushes; the other, the brush with which he was engaged. He accentuated the metre of his music by touches of paint on the drawing before him.

Then it seemed that the necessary inspiration struck me like a blow. Here were painter and pineapple in juxtaposition. They had approached each other more nearly than had ever happened until that moment. Only some two hundred feet of vertical space separated them. And I felt that these two entities—the one precious in my esteem, and the other evil—must now conjoin and complete their predestined state in contact each with other.

It was at this moment that my own volition left me, and a Thing-not-myself took the helm of my life, and steered me forward. With a power of resolution very different from that possessed by my own, with a decision and grip and masculine vigour remote from my vacillation and fickleness, my brain determined, and my hand leapt to obey the order. The crisis swept me like a storm. I felt as a watcher, chained and gagged, yet free to mark the action of another close at hand. I took the iron pineapple, held it perpendicularly above the head of the happy songster below, steadied my arm, that no tremor should deflect the missile, and dropped it.

The metal fell two hundred feet or more, and struck the exact centre of the grey hat beneath me. I heard the sound of impact—a dull thud muffled by the felt of the hat. But the consequences were terrific. Lightning had not destroyed the happy songster more instantly or more absolutely. His arms shot forth, his song was strangled in his head; his big body gave a convulsive jerk in every limb, and he fell forward upon his easel, and brought it to the ground beneath him.

From the moment that he crashed face down into the sand and shingle he remained motionless. In his hands were still the palette and single brush; his legs were drawn up stiffly in the attitude of a man swimming; as I watched, the blood began to well out of his head and run away into the ground. The iron pineapple had fallen forward, and was now a foot in front of him in the middle of his picture.

I descended to see what I had done. I felt a consciousness of immense relief and satisfaction. I was free—I was sane! The cloud had lifted from my spirit. I knew by an overwhelming conviction that henceforth and for ever I should find myself as other men.

I hastened down the cliff, stood on the deserted shore, and approached the fallen painter. It was not until my foot trampled the bloodstained sand at his ear that I began to apprehend the force of the thing that I had committed. The pathos exhibited by the figure of this stricken wretch impressed itself upon me. He was stout and elderly—older than I had guessed. Yet he had been singing of the joys of love; he had chanted the charm of a lady called 'Julia' when my iron pineapple descended, as the bolt of Jove from the sky, and struck him into senseless clay. His beard stuck out at a ridiculous angle from beneath his prone face, and my sense of decency led me to touch him, move him, and bestow his corpse in a manner more orderly.

I determined to turn him over, straighten out his legs, and not leave him thus, humped up on his belly like a frog that a wheel had crushed in the night.

But my purpose was frustrated, and that happened which cast me into an untold abyss of horror, and sent me flying as one demented from my murdered man. I touched his beard, and the whole mass of it came off in my hand! This incident, while less terrible indeed than other things that happened, yet sufficed to upset my jubilant brain. Its quality of unexpectedness may have caused my revulsion. I cannot say; but whereas I faced the dead without a tremor, and prepared reverently to bestow his palpitating dust, so that no feeling of the indecent or grotesque should grate upon the minds of his discoverers, now this outrageous and bizarre surrender of his beard at a touch struck me like the departing shadow of the madness I had dropped away for ever with the dropping of the stolen metal. I shivered, and I screamed aloud. My voice echoed along the cliff-face and climbed it, rang over the rocks, and floated seaward, where the broad foam-belts broke upon the shore. But none heard me save a hawk hovering aloft; none saw my frenzied act as I flung the great mass of hair from me and ran away.

Once, in that retreat, I turned and saw the hair, like some living, amorphous monster—a creature of the deep sea and darkness rather than of earth and light—creeping over the level sands after me. And then, indeed, I shrieked again, and sped for the cliffs and climbed a gully with such haste that my knees and knuckles were dripping blood before I reached the downs. Once there, I looked below in time to see the mass of hair caught up by the wind and blown afar into the sea.

That night I regained my peace, returned home, and slept as I had not slept for many years.

On the following day a West Country journal contained the following item of news:

'An occurrence fraught with the profoundest horror is reported from the holiday resort of Bude, and a spot associated with innocent pleasure, the happiness of children, and the rest and recuperation of jaded men of business, has suddenly become the sinister focus of an extraordinary and inexplicable crime. For the past six months a gentleman, named Walter Grant, has been residing in Victoria Road, at No. 9. The unfortunate artist—for such was his calling—devoted his attention to cliff scenery, and spent most of his time on Bude sands or in the immediate neighbourhood. And here he has mysteriously perished.'

The crime was then recorded, and the theory advanced that an iron pineapple found beside the dead man was responsible for his destruction. The fact that he had gone to paint with a beard, and been discovered a clean-shaven corpse was also noted. It was added that the man had displayed a kindly and courteous nature, and become popular among the few who had made his acquaintance. Inquiry established the fact that he was quite unknown in art circles, and that he had proposed to leave Bude on the Saturday that followed his death.

The incident of the recent robbery of the iron pineapple, and this, its sensational reappearance, also served to make exciting 'copy' for the papers; but a discovery which cast these trifles into the shade was destined next morning to fill not only our local journals. Then the English-speaking world discovered to its amazement that Bolsover Barbellion, the runaway rascal responsible for such widespread misery among the poor and needy, had been traced and discovered on the eve of his flight from England, and on the day after his flight from life. Not only the beard, but also the hair of the slain artist were discovered to be false, and investigations among his private papers established his identity beyond doubt.

A woman also came forward to testify it—a person named Julia Dalby. She and he were to have left England in a steamer from Plymouth on the Saturday after his departure from Bude, and she alone in the whole world knew his secret hiding-place. Their passages were already secured in the name of Mr and Mrs Grant, and they were about to sail for South America.

Not one shadow of suspicion ever fell upon me, but while my health was enormously improved, and my mind continued clear, my conscience was ill at ease, and the fact that my wife simply refused to credit the truth did not serve to lessen my unrest. A week after the actual event. I visited our minister, and designed to place the facts before him and invite his criticism and direction, but on the occasion of our meeting he was so much concerned about a private anxiety that I delayed my confession. He had determined that the corner-stone of our chapel must be extracted, for he held that no good would attend ministrations from a place of worship whose foundation had been laid by one of the greatest rascals recorded in modern history. The architect, however, demurred to this proposal, and submitted that to erase the inscription on the foundation-stone would surely meet the case. In grappling with this problem I forgot my own purpose of confession, and never more returned to it.

And today, sane and balanced of mind, I walk in the world of men and fear not the gaze of any fellow-creature. My life has taken a turn for the better; prosperity promises; the future never looked so fair. Above all, my mental balance is once more normal, and I enjoy a reputation for sound judgment and trustworthiness that brings my lesser neighbours to me in many of their difficulties.

And now I state the case against myself impartially and in print. I place myself without reserve at the mercy of man, and incidentally unravel a mystery that has puzzled the most astute intellects of our criminal service.

My theory—that for a fearful period I was the tool in Higher Hands, cannot, at least, be disproved, and I do not believe that any jury of my fellow-countrymen will condemn me to suffer for the part I played in the destruction of a most notorious enemy of society. Indeed, any earthly punishment would be an anti-climax and a jest at this hour. Nothing that wit of man might devise could put me again to the tortures of the days that are gone; or do more than reflect phantasmally the horror of the past.

GIVE ME MY TEETH—
GIVE ME MY TEETH

An old lady had been to church in the sands of Perranzabuloe. She found, amidst the numerous remains of mortality, some very good teeth. She pocketed these, and at night placed them on her dressing-table before getting into bed. She slept, but was at length disturbed by someone calling out, 'Give me my teeth—give me my teeth.' At first, the lady took no notice of this, but the cry, 'Give me my teeth,' was so constantly repeated, that at last, in terror, she jumped out of bed, took the teeth from the dressing-table and, opening the window, flung them out, exclaiming, 'Drat the teeth, take 'em.' They no sooner fell into the darkness on the road than hasty retreating footsteps were heard, and there were no more demands for the teeth.

ROBERT HUNT

WISH ME LUCK

H. A. MANHOOD

Eleven o'clock. The prim smell of Sunday was almost gone. Old Alice Pomeroy sat contentedly before a humming fire in the back parlour of the 'True-as-Stated,' talking quietly, noddingly, with her daughter-in-law, the young and sturdy wife of the absent landlord, sipping her nightly glass of a juniper punch called 'Sweet Emily,' perhaps because it was always brewed in a smoky brown cloam jug shaped like a caped maid.

A tabby cat rubbed solemnly against her clubbed foot as if seeking to heal it by sympathetic touch. The fire, a fighting huddle of salt timbers, sparked riotously, shaming the hanging lamp in whose glass belly the wick lay like a miserably bottled snake. China and hanging crystals glinted in a mock splintering and a ship in a bottle seemed caught in a tropic storm. Shadows flickered in dolphin-play across the low ceiling, their antics interesting the several portraits on the wall so that they lived again briefly, nodding amusedly to each other. Supper waited at one end of the scrubbed table; cold meat, bread and pickles and a flat saffron cake, knife-stamped with a large dee, a great cruet standing like a guardhouse in the middle.

Susan, with the help of dumb Meg, the lank, worm-lipped house-girl, had long ago tidied the bar-room and was waiting restlessly for the return of Dan Pomeroy, her husband, whom she loved deeply and deservedly with a generosity equalling his own.

Dan, following the recent death of his father and at his mother's wish, had but lately returned from America with a sensible fortune of his own and a sizeable first nugget on his watch-chain. The prospect of a gentlemanly landlording in the place of his birth pleased him very well. What better frame for the rest of his life than the 'True-as-Stated' in Tuffrand Cove? A neat stone house, tight as a whelk in its place on the quay; sea and wind and shining sand and gulls galore and the moors and cliffs with hares and wildfowl for coursing and shooting. And for a wife a darling girl of the place with money in her own right and no need for crawl or quarrel between them. Here, indeed, was heaven as you make it and no mistake!

A fine figure of a Cornishman, travelled and full of a merry knowledge and sympathy, Dan's coming had provided the Cove with some amusement for, with his fine black beard and moustaches, he was the living image of Squire Haddicoat, owner of the village and twenty thousand acres besides. A small thing, you'd think, but the autocratic Squire wasn't pleased.

Not that Dan minded one scrap. Broad-mindedly he felt that he was as entitled to wear a beard as any rural lord and it only amused him when folk mistook him for a squire become genial.

Twice the Squire sent brisk word that he trusted that Dan would shave and end an unbecoming mockery. But Dan didn't see why at all. If m'lord didn't like it, well, let him part with his own beard. Which sensible refusal upset the Squire badly. Uncommonly wealthy, he was but rarely thwarted. His father and grandfather had been powerful and bearded before him, and tradition couldn't be broken.

Full power of damnation had been his till now, but in this case the power had failed lamentably, and, since the Pomeroys owned the 'True-as-Stated' and sold the best liquor in twenty miles, there seemed nothing he could do to force obedience. He was accustomed to ride about the countryside in a shiny dandy cart with a spanking, pampered thoroughbred between the shafts, and Dan, just because it suited him and out of no malice, used a raddled ass-cart and one of the unkempt, shore-grazing asses so cherished by his mother.

Naturally the Squire took his riding in this manner as an added insult, and he schemed viciously to force Dan out of the parish. But Dan was within his rights and couldn't be hit in the pocket or anywhere else. He just went his own laughing way, preaching a bit, too, sometimes, telling what he'd seen of the beauty of earth, and that we'd enjoy it the more if we didn't crave for power or undue riches or for the beauty of a heaven which wasn't there. Which only increased Squire Haddicoat's anger and added to the jest as the villagers saw it.

Sitting with her glass held close to her stern, whiskered chin, her tight grey hair like a cap of silver, Old Alice gave gossip as she had heard it that day across the bar, Susan listening indignantly.

'What right has he to play the king?'

'No right at all,' Alice answered her, sad and cross, too, to think of a blindness where clear vision should have been; 'but then, right can't be measured, for it changes weight with every one of us. If we could all agree on right and wrong half the world would be out of work, and that would be wrong to start with. 'Tis strife, after all, that's the salt of living for most, and God bless the boldest.'

'More's the pity.'

Old Alice nodded sagely: 'A whining pity, so 'tis, and no sense or good even if the Squire does choose to make a whole seething sermon out of a simple, no-matter likeness. "Those that mock shall be trampled, so sayeth the Lord" . . . that's the way he clamoured in the House today, so they say, fierce as Moses, and the Parson upholding him for fear he'd lose the living. Snooks to him, I say, and best maybe if we say naught to Dan about it.'

Susan shrugged, parting the heavy curtains, staring out across the bay: 'I wish Dan would come,' she said softly. 'It shouldn't take him this long to drive home from Muryan, with a moon, too.'

'Don't worry, child,' Old Alice soothed her smilingly, pleased to think that Dan had such a good reason for hurry. Life had come sweet for them all, like a flower after a struggle.

To Susan the moon seemed very big and bright, slipping with plump good-humour through lacy folds of cloud, causing the sea to glimmer like a ploughing of sheer frost. The blinking harbour light was like a tiny pulsing wound in the dreaming flesh of earth and distant lights, sparking as if in sympathy, seemed to hobble nearer like cripples in excited action.

The carns loomed like great bible waves, just as if the tin mines beneath had sucked in a great, unsettling breath of air. It was very quiet after the Christmas gales, only the surf rasping like the breath of a sleeper. The air, unhurried, was alive with a purpose of its own, pure and lovely. Soon a right breeze would bring the mimosa sweetness of the Scillies like love to the mainland and the moorlands and valleys, even the stone edges would flower responsively, amazingly.

Spring already in her heart, Susan smiled to think of Dan

driving along the high and lonely road across the stone-crumped moor, past rock-pools gleaming like the drip of stars and the huddled gorse brakes, moaning everlastingly as if with the pain of the birth of thorns. He'd be thinking all that she was thinking, his hat tipped back and a tiny, merry whistle on his lips, a pirate at ease on a skimming splinter as he'd say. Maybe he'd stopped at the carpenter's shop, way up at the crossroads, for a word with blind Pengelly and his son about a boat 'for my wife and meself to be sailing' . . . bless him!

Her mind vivid with love, it was easy for Susan to imagine the shop standing like an ark left high and dry after the falling of the waters and the tenants still amazed at salvation; lonely and with only an enormous chiselled guide-stone, old as comfort, for company.

Pengelly's reason for building there had been uncommonly good. A ship's carpenter in his youth, he had once been wrecked on a shark's tooth of an island in the tropics, suffering great thirst before rescue. Home again, he had remembered the unfailing spring at the crossways, the craggy-rocked basin bottomed with fine silver sand through which water bubbled ceaselessly, airily, as might the breath of a hidden monster, the sand spurting and dancing waywardly. A good reason for building. At night the long, faintly sand-frosted windows of the ship glimmered yellowly like the scuttles of a ghost ship.

The door was thick-crusted with paint, for young Pengelly tried out his colours on it, colours for boats and cradles: they made coffins, too; they should be coloured also, black for the likes of Squire Haddicoat, sky-blue or sun-colour for Dan. . . .

Susan smiled, driving away the gruesome thought, touching her throat gently where Dan had so often kissed and nibbled it, and Old Alice, watching, smiled too, and thought she would be going aloft to her bed for it would be better for love to be alone and waiting for its likeness. In the outer bar-room a tap dripped as if marking a time of its own, and Alice felt that time did indeed run differently in the 'True-as-Stated,' and she thanked God for the harmony, that Dan had come home to her and married so well and faithfully.

Rising stiffly on her great stick, her club-foot dragging, she nodded towards the portrait of her husband as she always did, her thin Spanish face wrinkling wisely and affectionately. But, even as she did so, Susan moved at the window, holding a finger for silence. Like bouncing stones in the stillness came the sound of hooves down the hill.

'He's surely making up for lost time!' Susan hurried to the door, anxious to help Dan with his stabling.

But Alice still listened, quick to notice differences: 'Too leapy for Dan,' she muttered, and reached for her shawl, pinning it fast with the air of one going to battle. Trouble had never yet caught her unawares. A late-running horse meant something unpleasant in her experience, a call for the doctor or something similar. A tiny fear snatched at her heart, but she put it bravely aside. Wheels bumped on the cobbles and, almost at once, there was a rapping on the front door. A dog barked near at hand and a voice damned it.

'Squire Haddicoat!' Old Alice sucked apprehensively, following Susan through the doorway, the gaping Meg after her, her hands wrapped in her apron. The sweating horse backed nervously as they turned the corner, but an angry word from the Squire checked it. He was knocking again at the door with the butt of his whip as he sat.

'Well?' Old Alice lost no time.

Squire Haddicoat lowered his whip, teeth grinning sourly white in his beard.

'There has been an accident. I ran into Pomeroy on the hill. My horse was scared and trampled down on him. You had better go and look.'

Susan said nothing. Her eyes widened with sudden fear. Catching at Meg she ran with her away up the hill, their shadows grotesque in the moonlight. Old Alice stood grimly, resting on her stick, breathing hard. She thought of Dan dead through malice, remembering queerly the agony of his birth so long ago. Her thoughts spun crazily, then righted themselves, settling icily. A strength came to her as if her dead husband were warm and living at her side. 'Accident be damned,' she thought. The Squire was watching her amusedly, pleased to have settled a score. Recovered, Alice bobbed her head cunningly:

'Thank you for bringing the news. It must have shaken you a bit. I'll get some brandy. . . .'

It was on the tip of the Squire's tongue to tell her to go to hell; he'd slammed the old harridan's son as he deserved, but it wouldn't do for the old crow to guess that he'd done it deliberately. It would be prudent to humour her.

'If it won't be troubling you too much,' he said with cynical politeness. A tot would certainly be acceptable after that trampling. Just like a damned grinning evil reflection of himself the fellow had been, God rot him! No one would dare to accuse him of criminal malice, especially after the kindly way he'd brought the news.

Grimly Old Alice hobbled back into the house, returning with a bottle of brandy and a glass. The glass she filled and handed to the Squire.

'Wish me luck!' she said.

Off-handedly the Squire did so, drinking appreciatively and, as his head tipped, Old Alice braced herself, lifting her heavy stick, swinging it hard on the back of his neck above the astrakhan collar. Gruntingly he flopped forward, the glass falling splinteringly. Swiftly Alice swamped brandy over him, ramming the bottle into his pocket.

Then she used her stick again, this time upon the horse so that it lunged and galloped madly along the quay. Alice waited. The horse reared on the brink, but too late to prevent a fall. There was a wrenching crash and splash. Then complete silence. Knowing the way of the rocks under the quay, Alice did not need to doubt. Carefully rubbing the knob of her stick on her shawl she went back into the house, standing before the portrait of her husband, drawing comfort from his calm, approving gaze. A rub of spirit on her bloodless cheeks and she hurried through the village to the house of the doctor, knocking him up.

'Hurry! Hurry! A terrible mess. Our Dan trampled. Squire Haddicoat raving drunk and fallen over the quay . . . Don't bother about your tie, man!'

Stiff-lipped in her fear, Old Alice hurried pantingly back, her stick banging loudly on the cobbles. If Dan was gone the sun might just as well be dead too. Meg and Susan were pulling the broken-shafted ass-cart to the door of the 'True-as-Stated.'

Dan lay limply, bloody-cheeked. Susan was white-faced, wooden-fingered in her misery. Meg gabbled and clucked excitedly. Gently the three of them carried Dan into the house, Alice finding a special brandy, pouring water. Susan lifted the heavy head, opening the tight, full lips, the brandy glass rattling against the wide, lucky teeth . . . please God, their luck held good this time. Lightly she dabbed at the slashed flesh, listening, nodding tremulously, whispering in her relief.

'It's all right.'

'God be praised!'

Old Alice unlocked her hands thankfully, hobbling to a seat, very tired and grateful, without regret. Meg bubbled noisily as she unlaced Dan's boots. A little more brandy and Dan gulped and sighed and blinked, struggling weakly upright. Aware of Susan and his mother, he grimaced quaintly:

'A bit of an accident,' he said.

'Accident?'

Dan was forced to admit that it was hardly that.

Old Alice nodded contentedly, smiling up at the portrait on the wall. Just like his father, Dan was, honest to a fault. Well, there'd be peace for all of them and no more malice. A pleasant gift. Wish me luck! Chuckling deeply, she blessed them all before hobbling away to bed.

THE HELL-HOUNDS

A poor herdsman was journeying homeward across the moors one windy night, when he heard at a distance among the Tors the baying of hounds, which he soon recognised as the dismal chorus of the dandy dogs. It was three or four miles to his house; and very much alarmed, he hurried onward as fast as the treacherous nature of the soil and the uncertainty of the path would allow; but, alas! the melancholy yelping of the hounds, and the dismal holloa of the hunter came nearer and nearer. After a considerable run, they had so gained upon him, that on looking back—oh horror! he could distinctly see hunter and dogs. The former was terrible to look at, and had the usual complement of saucer-eyes, horns, and tail, accorded by common consent to the legendary devil. He was black of course, and carried in his hand a long hunting-pole. The dogs, a numerous pack, blackened the small patch of moor that was visible; each snorting fire, and uttering a yelp of indescribably frightful tone. No cottage, rock, or tree was near to give the herdsman shelter, and nothing apparently remained to him but to abandon himself to their fury, when a happy thought suddenly flashed upon him and suggested a resource. Just as they were about to rush upon him, he fell on his knees in prayer. There was strange power in the holy words he uttered; for immediately, as if resistance had been offered, the hell-hounds stood at bay, howling more dismally than ever, and the hunter shouted, 'Bo Shrove', which (says my informant) means in the old language, 'The Boy Prays', at which they all drew off on some other pursuit and disappeared.

From FOLK LORE OF A CORNISH VILLAGE
by T. Q. COUCH

MRS LUNT

SIR HUGH WALPOLE

I

'Do you believe in ghosts?' I asked Runciman. I had to ask him this very platitudinous question more because he was so difficult a man to spend an hour with rather than for any other reason. You know his books, perhaps, or more probably you don't know them—*The Running Man, The Elm Tree*, and *Crystal and Candlelight*. He is one of those little men who are constant enough in this age of immense overproduction of books, men who publish every autumn their novel, who arouse by that publication in certain critics eager appreciation and praise, who have a small and faithful public, whose circulation is very small indeed, who, when you meet them, have little to say, are often shy and nervous, pessimistic and remote from daily life. Such men do fine work, are made but little of in their own day, and perhaps fifty years after their death are rediscovered by some digging critic and become a sort of cult with a new generation.

I asked Runciman that question because, for some unknown reason, I had invited him to dinner at my flat, and was now faced with a long evening filled with that most tiresome of all conversations, talk that dies every two minutes and has to be revived with terrific exertions. Being myself a critic, and having on many occasions praised Runciman's work, he was the more nervous and shy with me; had I abused it, he would perhaps have had plenty to say—he was that kind of man. But my question was a lucky one: it roused him instantly, his long, bony body became full of a new energy, his eyes stared into a rich and exciting reminiscence, he spoke without pause, and I took care not to interrupt him. He certainly told me one of the most astounding stories I have ever heard. Whether it was true or not I cannot, of course, say. These ghost stories are nearly always at second or third hand. I had, at any rate, the good fortune to secure mine from the source. Moreover, Runciman was not a liar; he was too serious for that. He himself admitted that he was not sure, at this distance of time, as to whether the thing had gained as the years passed. However, here it is as he told it.

'It was some fifteen years ago,' he said. 'I went down to Cornwall to stay with Robert Lunt. Do you remember his name? No, I suppose you do not. He wrote several novels; some of those half-and-half things that are not quite novels, not quite poems, rather mystical and picturesque, and are the very devil to do well. De la Mare's *Return* is a good example of the kind of thing. I had reviewed somewhere his last book, and reviewed it favourably, and received from him a really touching letter showing that the man was thirsting for praise, and also, I fancied, for company. He lived in Cornwall somewhere on the sea-coast, and his wife had died some two years before; he said he was quite alone there, and would I come and spend Christmas with him; he hoped I would not think this impertinent; he expected that I would be engaged already, but he could not resist the chance. Well, I wasn't engaged; far from it. If Lunt was lonely, so was I; if Lunt was a failure, so was I; I was touched, as I have said, by his letter, and I accepted his invitation. As I went down in the train to Penzance I wondered what kind of man he would be. I had never seen any photographs of him; he was not the sort of author whose picture the newspapers publish. He must be, I fancied, about my own age—perhaps rather older. I know when we're lonely how some of us are for ever imagining that a friend will somewhere turn up, that ideal friend who will understand all one's feelings, who will give one affection without being sentimental, who will take an interest in one's affairs without being impertinent—yes, the sort of friend one never finds.

'I fancy that I became quite romantic about Lunt before I reached Penzance. We could talk, he and I, about all those literary questions that seemed to me at that time so absorbing; we would perhaps often stay together and even travel abroad on those little journeys that are so swiftly melancholy when one is alone, so delightful when one has a perfect companion. I imagined him as sparse and delicate and refined, with a sort of wistfulness and rather childish play of fancy. We had both, so far, failed in our careers, but perhaps together we would do great things.

'When I arrived at Penzance it was almost dark, and

the snow, threatened all day by an overhanging sky, had begun gently and timorously to fall. He had told me in his letter that a fly would be at the station to take me to his house; and there I found it—a funny old weather-beaten carriage with a funny old weather-beaten driver. At this distance of time my imagination may have created many things, but I fancy that from the moment I was shut into that carriage some dim suggestion of fear and apprehension attacked me. I fancy that I had some absurd impulse to get out of the thing and take the night train back to London again—an action that would have been very unlike me, as I had always a sort of obstinate determination to carry through anything that I had begun. In any case, I was uncomfortable in that carriage; it had, I remember, a nasty, musty smell of damp straw and stale eggs, and it seemed to confine me so closely as though it were determined that, once I was in, I should never get out again. Then, it was bitterly cold; I was colder during that drive than I have ever been before or since. It was that penetrating cold that seems to pierce your very brain, so that I could not think with any clearness, but only wish again and again that I hadn't come. Of course, I could see nothing—only feel the jolt over the uneven road—and once and again we seemed to fight our way through dark paths, because I could feel the overhanging branches of the trees knock against the cab with mysterious taps, as though they were trying to give me some urgent message.

'Well, I mustn't make more of it than the facts allow, and I mustn't see into it all the significance of the events that followed. I only know that as the drive proceeded I became more and more miserable: miserable with the cold of my body, the misgivings of my imagination, the general loneliness of my case.

'At last we stopped. The old scarecrow got slowly off his box, with many heavings and sighings, came to the cab door and, with great difficulty and irritating slowness, opened it. I got out of it, and found that the snow was now falling very heavily indeed, and that the path was lightened with its soft, mysterious glow. Before me was a humped and ungainly shadow: the house that was to receive me. I could make nothing of it in that darkness, but only stood there shivering while the old man pulled at the door-bell with a sort of frantic energy as though he were anxious to be rid of the whole job as quickly as possible and return to his own place. At last, after what seemed an endless time, the door opened, and an old man, who might have been own brother to the driver, poked out his head. The two old men talked together, and at last my bag was shouldered and I was permitted to come in out of the piercing cold.

'Now this, I know, is not imagination. I have never at any period of my life hated at first sight so vigorously any dwelling-place into which I have ever entered as I did that house. There was nothing especially disagreeable about my first vision of the hall. It was a large, dark place, lit by two dim lamps, cold and cheerless; but I got no particular impression of it because at once I was conducted out of it, led along a passage, and then introduced into a room which was, I saw at once, as warm and comfortable as the hall had been dark and dismal. I was, in fact, so eagerly pleased at the large and leaping fire that I moved towards it at once, not noting, at the first moment, the presence of my host; and when I did see him I could not believe that it was he. I have told you the kind of man that I had expected; but, instead of the sparse, sensitive artist, I found facing me a large, burly man, over six foot, I should fancy, as broad-shouldered as he was tall, giving evidence of great muscular strength, the lower part of his face hidden by a black, pointed beard.

'But if I was astonished at the sight of him, I was doubly amazed when he spoke. His voice was thin and piping, like that of some old woman, and the little nervous gestures that he made with his hands were even more feminine than his voice. But I had to allow, perhaps, for excitement, for excited he was; he came up to me, took my hand in both of his, and held it as though he would never let it go. In the evening, when we sat over our port, he apologized for this. "I was so glad to see you," he said; "I couldn't believe that really you would come; you are the first visitor of my own kind that I have had here for ever so long. I was ashamed, indeed, of asking you, but I had to snatch at the chance—it means so much to me."

'His eagerness, in fact, had something disturbing about it; something pathetic, too. He simply couldn't do too much for me: he led me through funny crumbling old passages, the boards creaking under us at every step, up some dark stairs, the walls hung, so far as I could see in the dim light, with faded yellow photographs of places, and showed me into my room with a deprecating agitated gesture as though he expected me at the first sight of it to turn and run. I didn't like it any more than I liked the rest of the house; but that was not my host's fault. He had done everything he possibly could for me: there was a large fire flaming in the open fireplace, there was a hot bottle, as he explained to me, in the big four-poster bed, and the old man who had opened the door to me was already taking my clothes out of my bag and putting them away. Lunt's nervousness was almost sentimental. He put both his hands on my shoulders and said, looking at me pleadingly: "If you only knew what it is for me to have you here, the talks we'll have. Well, well, I must leave you. You'll come down and join me, won't you, as soon as you can?"

'It was then, when I was left alone in my room, that I had my second impulse to flee. Four candles in tall old silver candlesticks were burning brightly, and these, with the blazing fire, gave plenty of light; and yet the room was in some way dim, as though a faint smoke pervaded it, and I remember that I went to one of the old lattice windows and threw it open for a moment as though I felt stifled. Two things quickly made me close it. One was the intense cold which, with a fluttering scamper of snow, blew into the room; the other was the quite deafening roar of the sea, which seemed to fling itself at my very face as though it wanted to knock me down. I quickly shut the window, turned round, and saw an old woman standing just inside the door. Now every story of this kind depends for its interest on its verisimilitude. Of course, to make my tale convincing I should be able to prove to you that I saw that old woman; but I can't. I can only urge upon you my rather dreary reputation of probity. You know that I'm a teetotaller, and always have been, and, most important evidence of all, I was not expecting to see an old woman; and yet I hadn't the least doubt in the world but that it was an old woman I saw. You may talk about shadows, clothes hanging on the back of the door, and the rest of it. I don't know. I've no theories about this story, I'm not a spiritualist, I don't know that I believe in anything especially, except the beauty of beautiful things.

'We'll put it, if you like, that I fancied that I saw an old woman, and my fancy was so strong that I can give you to this day a pretty detailed account of her appearance. She wore a black silk dress and on her breast was a large, ugly gold brooch; she had black hair, brushed back from her forehead and parted down the middle; she wore a collar of some white stuff round her throat; her face was one of the wickedest, most malignant, and furtive that I have ever seen—very white in colour. She was shrivelled enough now, but might once have been rather beautiful. She stood there quietly, her hands at her side. I thought that she was some kind of housekeeper. "I have everything I want, thank you," I said. "What a splendid fire!" I turned for a moment towards it, and when I looked back she was gone. I thought nothing of this, of course, but drew up an old chair covered with green faded tapestry, and thought that I would read a little from some book that I had brought down with me before I went to join my host. The fact was that I was not very intent upon joining him before I must. I didn't like him. I had already made up my mind that I would find some excuse to return to London as soon as possible. I can't tell you why I didn't like him, except that I was myself very reserved and had, like many Englishmen, a great distrust of demonstrations, especially from another man. I hadn't cared for the way in which he had put his hands on my shoulders, and I felt perhaps that I wouldn't be able to live up to all his eager excitement about me.

'I sat in my chair and took up my book, but I had not been reading for more than two minutes before I was conscious of a most unpleasant smell. Now, there are all sorts of smells—healthy and otherwise—but I think the nastiest is that chilly kind of odour that comes from bad sanitation and stuffy rooms combined; you meet it sometimes at little country inns and decrepit town lodgings. This smell was so definite that I could almost locate it; it came from near the door. I got up, approached the door, and at once it was as though I were drawing near to somebody who, if you'll forgive the impoliteness, was not accustomed to taking too many baths. I drew back just as I might had an actual person been there. Then quite suddenly the smell was gone, the room was fresh, and I saw, to my surprise, that one of the windows had opened and that snow was again blowing in. I closed it and went downstairs.

'The evening that followed was odd enough. My host

was not in himself an unlikeable man; he did his very utmost to please me. He had a fine culture and a wide knowledge of books and things. He became quite cheerful as the evening went on; gave me a good dinner in a funny little old dining-room hung with some admirable mezzotints. The old serving man looked after us—a funny old man, with a long white beard like a goat—and, oddly enough, it was from him that I first recaught my earlier apprehension. He had just put the dessert on the table, had arranged my plate in front of me, when I saw him give a start and look towards the door. My attention was attracted to this because his hand, as it touched the plate, suddenly trembled. My eyes followed, but I could see nothing. That he was frightened of something was perfectly clear, and then (it may, of course, very easily have been fancy) I thought that I detected once more that strange unwholesome smell.

'I forgot this again when we were both seated in front of a splendid fire in the library. Lunt had a very fine collection of books, and it was delightful to him, as it is to every book-collector, to have somebody with him who could really appreciate them. We stood looking at one book after another and talking eagerly about some of the minor early English novelists who were my especial hobby—Bage, Godwin, Henry Mackenzie, Mrs Shelley, Mat Lewis, and others—when once again he affected me most unpleasantly by putting his arm round my shoulders. I have all my life disliked intensely to be touched by certain people. I suppose we all feel like this. It is one of those inexplicable things; and I disliked this so much that I abruptly drew away.

'Instantly he was changed into a man of furious and ungovernable rage; I thought that he was going to strike me. He stood there quivering all over, the words pouring out of his mouth incoherently, as though he were mad and did not know what he was saying. He accused me of insulting him, of abusing his hospitality, of throwing his kindness back into his face, and of a thousand other ridiculous things; and I can't tell you how strange it was to hear all this coming out in that shrill piping voice as though it were from an agitated woman, and yet to see with one's eyes that big, muscular frame, those immense shoulders, and that dark bearded face.

'I said nothing. I am, physically, a coward. I dislike, above anything else in the world, any sort of quarrel. At last

I brought out, "I am very sorry. I didn't mean anything. Please forgive me," and then hurriedly turned to leave the room. At once he changed again; now he was almost in tears. He implored me not to go; said it was his wretched temper, but that he was so miserable and unhappy, and had for so long now been alone and desolate that he hardly knew what he was doing. He begged me to give him another chance, and if I would only listen to his story I would perhaps be more patient with him.

'At once, so oddly is man constituted, I changed in my feelings towards him. I was very sorry for him. I saw that he was a man on the edge of his nerves, and that he really did need some help and sympathy, and would be quite distracted if he could not get it. I put my hand on his shoulder to quieten him and to show him that I bore no malice, and I felt that his great body was quivering from head to foot. We sat down again, and in an odd, rambling manner he told me his story. It amounted to very little, and the gist of it was that, rather to have some sort of companionship than from any impulse of passion, he had married, some fifteen years before, the daughter of a neighbouring clergyman. They had had no very happy life together, and at the last, he told me quite frankly, he had hated her. She had been mean, overbearing, and narrow-minded; it had been, he confessed, nothing but a relief to him when, just a year ago, she had suddenly died from heart failure. He had thought then that things would go better with him, but they had not; nothing had gone right with him since. He hadn't been able to work, many of his friends had ceased to come to see him, he had found it even difficult to get servants to stay with him, he was desperately lonely, he slept badly—that was why his temper was so terribly on edge.

'He had no one in the house with him save the old man, who was, fortunately, an excellent cook, and a boy—the old man's grandson. "Oh, I thought," I said, "that that excellent meal tonight was cooked by your housekeeper." "My housekeeper?" he answered. "There's no woman in the house." "Oh, but one came to my room," I replied, "this evening—an old lady-like looking person in a black silk dress." "You were mistaken," he answered in the oddest voice, as though he were exerting all the strength that he possessed to keep himself quiet and controlled. "I am sure that I saw her," I answered. "There couldn't be any mistake." And I described her to him. "You were mistaken," he repeated again. "Don't you see that you must have been when I tell you there is no woman in the house?" I reassured him quickly lest there should be another outbreak of rage. Then there followed the oddest kind of appeal. Urgently, as though his very life depended upon it, he begged me to stay with him for a few days. He implied, although he said nothing definitely, that he was in great trouble, that if only I would stay for a few days all would be well, that if ever in all my life I had had a chance of doing a kind action I had one now, that he couldn't expect me to stop in so dreary a place, but that he would never forget it if I did. He spoke in a voice of such urgent distress that I reassured him as I might a child, promising that I would stay, and shaking hands with him on it as though it were a kind of solemn oath between us.

II

'I am sure that you would wish me to give you this incident as it occurred, and if the final catastrophe seems to come, as it were, accidentally, I can only say to you that that was how it happened. It is since the event that I have tried to put two and two together, and that they don't altogether make four is the fault that mine shares, I suppose, with every true ghost story.

'But the truth is that after that very strange episode between us I had a very good night. I slept the sleep of all justice, cosy and warm, in my four-poster, with the murmur of the sea beyond the windows to rock my slumbers. Next morning, too, was bright and cheerful, the sun sparkling down on the snow, and the snow sparkling back to the sun as though they were glad to see one another. I had a very pleasant morning looking at Lunt's books, talking to him, and writing one or two letters. I must say that, after all, I liked the man. His appeal to me on the night before had touched me. So few people, you see, had ever appealed to me about anything. His nervousness was there and the constant sense of apprehension, yet he seemed to be putting the best face on it, doing his utmost to set me at my ease in order to induce me to stay, I suppose, and to give him a little of that company that he so terribly needed. I dare say if I had not been so busy about the books I would not have been so happy. There was a strange eerie silence about that house if one ever stopped to listen; and once, I remember, sitting at the old bureau writing a letter, I raised my head and looked up, and caught Lunt watching as though he wondered whether I had heard or noticed anything. And so I listened too, and it seemed to me as though someone were on the other side of the library door with their hand raised to knock; a quaint notion, with nothing to support it, but I could have sworn that if I had gone to the door and opened it suddenly someone would have been there.

'However I was cheerful enough, and after lunch quite happy. Lunt asked me if I would like a walk, and I said I would; and we started out in the sunshine over the crunching snow towards the sea. I don't remember of what we talked; we seemed to be now quite at our ease with one another. We crossed the fields to a certain point, looked down at the sea—smooth now, like silk—and turned back. I remember that I was so cheerful that I seemed suddenly to take a happy view of all my prospects. I began to confide in Lunt, telling him of my little plans, of my hopes for the book that I was then writing, and even began rather timidly to suggest to him that perhaps we should do something together; that what we both needed was a friend of common taste with ourselves. I know that I was talking on, that we had crossed a little village street, and were turning up the path towards the dark avenue of trees that led to his house, when suddenly the change came.

'What I first noticed was that he was not listening to me; his gaze was fixed beyond me, into the very heart of the black clump of trees that fringed the silver landscape. I looked too, and my heart bounded. There, standing just in front of the trees, as though she were waiting for us, was the old woman whom I had seen in my room the night before. I stopped. "Why, there she is!" I said. "That's the old woman of whom I was speaking—the old woman who came to my room." He caught my shoulder with his hand. "There's nothing there," he said. "Don't you see that that's shadow? What's the matter with you? Can't you see that there's nothing?" I stepped forward, and there was nothing, and

I wouldn't, to this day, be able to tell you whether it was hallucination or not. I can only say that, from that moment, the afternoon appeared to become dark.

'As we entered into the avenue of trees, silently and hurrying as though someone were behind us, the dusk seemed to have fallen so that I could scarcely see my way. We reached the house breathless. He hastened into his study as though I were not with him, but I followed and, closing the door behind me, said, with all the force that I had at command: "Now, what is this? What is it that's troubling you? You must tell me! How can I help you if you don't?" And he replied, in so strange a voice that it was as though he had gone out of his mind: "I tell you there's nothing! Can't you believe me when I tell you there's nothing at all? I'm quite all right. . . . Oh, my God!—my God! . . . don't leave me! . . . This is the very day—the very night she said . . . But I did nothing, I tell you—I did nothing—it's only her beastly malice. . . ." He broke off. He still held my arm with his hand. He made strange movements, wiping his forehead as though it were damp with sweat, almost pleading with me; then suddenly angry again, then beseeching once more, as though I had refused him the one thing he wanted.

'I saw that he was truly not far from madness, and I began myself to have a sudden terror of this damp, dark house, this great, trembling man, and something more that was worse than they. But I pitied him. How could you or any man have helped it? I made him sit down in the arm-chair beside the fire, which had now dwindled to a few glimmering red coals. I let him hold me close to him with his arm and clutch my hand with his, and I repeated, as quiet as I might: "But tell me; don't be afraid, whatever it is you have done. Tell me what danger it is you fear, and then we can face it together." "Fear! fear!" he repeated; and then, with a mighty effort which I could not but admire, he summoned all his control. "I'm off my head," he said, "with loneliness and depression. My wife died a year ago on this very night. We hated one another. I couldn't be sorry when she died, and she knew it. When that last heart attack came on, between her gasps she told me that she would return, and I've always dreaded this night. That's partly why I asked you to come, to have anyone here, anybody, and you've been very kind—more kind than I had any right to expect.

You must think me insane going on like this, but see me through tonight and we'll have splendid times together. Don't desert me now—now, of all times!" I promised that I would not. I soothed him as best I could. We sat there, for I know not how long, through the gathering dark; we neither of us moved, the fire died out, and the room was lit with a strange dim glow that came from the snowy landscape beyond the uncurtained windows. Ridiculous, perhaps, as I look back at it. We sat there, I in a chair close to his, hand in hand, like a couple of lovers; but, in real truth, two men terrified, fearful of what was coming, and unable to do anything to meet it.

'I think that that was perhaps the strangest part of it; a sort of paralysis that crept over me. What would you or anyone else have done—summoned the old man, gone down to the village inn, fetched the local doctor? I could do nothing but see the snow-shine move like trembling water about the furniture and hear, through the urgent silence, the faint hoot of an owl from the trees in the wood.

III

'Oddly enough, I can remember nothing, try as I may, between that strange vigil and the moment when I myself, wakened out of a brief sleep, sat up in bed to see Lunt standing inside my room holding a candle. He was wearing a nightshirt, and looked huge in the candlelight, his black beard falling intensely dark on the white stuff of his shirt. He came very quietly towards my bed, the candle throwing flickering shadows about the room. When he spoke it was in a voice low and subdued, almost a whisper. "Would you come," he asked, "only for half an hour—just for half an hour?" he repeated, staring at me as though he didn't know me. "I'm unhappy without somebody—very unhappy." Then he looked over his shoulder, held the candle high above his head, and stared piercingly at every part of the room. I could see that something had happened to him, that he had taken another step into the country of Fear—a step that had withdrawn him from me and from every other human being. He whispered: "When you come, tread softly; I don't want anyone to hear us." I did what I could. I got out of bed, put on my dressing-gown and slippers, and tried to persuade him to stay with me. The fire was almost dead, but I told him that we would build it up again, and that we would sit there and wait for the morning; but no, he repeated again and again: "It's better in my own room; we're safer there." "Safe from what?" I asked him, making him look at me. "Lunt, wake up! You're as though you were asleep. There's nothing to fear. We've nobody but ourselves. Stay here and let us talk, and have done with this nonsense." But he wouldn't answer; only drew me forward down the dark passage, and then turned into his room, beckoning me to follow. He got into bed and sat hunched up there, his hands holding his knees, staring at the door, and every once and again shivering with a little tremor. The only light in the room was that from the candle, now burning low, and the only sound was the purring whisper of the sea.

'It seemed to make little difference to him that I was there. He did not look at me, but only at the door, and when I spoke to him he did not answer me nor seem to hear what I had said. I sat down beside the bed and, in order to break the silence, talked on about anything, about nothing, and was dropping off, I think, into a confused doze, when I heard his voice breaking across mine. Very clearly and distinctly he said: "If I killed her, she deserved it; she was never a good wife to me, not from the first; she shouldn't have irritated me as she did—she knew what my temper was. She had a worse one than mine, though. She can't touch me; I'm as strong as she is." And it was then, as clearly as I can now remember, that his voice suddenly sank into a sort of gentle whisper, as though he were almost glad that his fears had been confirmed. He whispered: "She's there!" I cannot possibly describe to you how that whisper seemed to let Fear loose like water through my body. I could see nothing—the candle was flaming high in the last moment of its life—I could see nothing; but Lunt suddenly screamed, with a shrill cry like a tortured animal in agony: "Keep her off me, keep her away from me, keep her off—keep her off!" He caught me, his hands digging into my shoulders; then, with an awful effect of constricted muscles, as though rigor had caught and held him, his arms slowly fell away, he slipped back on to the bed as though someone were pushing him, his hands fell against the sheet, his whole body jerked with a convulsive effort, and then he rolled over. I saw nothing; only quite distinctly in my nostrils was that same fetid odour that I had known on the preceding evening. I rushed to the door, opened it, shouted down the long passage again and again, and soon the old man came running. I sent him for the doctor, and then could not return to the room, but stood there listening, hearing nothing save the whisper of the sea, the loud ticking of the hall clock. I flung open the window at the end of the passage; the sea rushed in with its precipitant roar; some bells chimed the hour. Then at last, beating into myself more courage, I turned back towards the room. . . .'

'Well?' I asked as Runciman paused. 'He was dead, of course?'

'Dead, the doctor afterwards said, of heart failure.'

'Well?' I asked again.

'That's all.' Runciman paused. 'I don't know whether you can even call it a ghost story. My idea of the old woman may have been all hallucination. I don't even know whether his wife was like that when she was alive. She may have been large and fat. Lunt died of an evil conscience.'

'Yes,' I said.

'The only thing,' Runciman added at last, after a long pause, 'is that on Lunt's body there were marks—on his neck especially, some on his chest—as of fingers pressing in, scratches and dull blue marks. He may, in his terror, have caught at his own throat. . . .'

'Yes,' I said again.

'Anyway'—Runciman shivered—'I don't like Cornwall—beastly country. Queer things happen there—something in the air. . . .'

'So I've heard,' I answered. 'And now have a drink. We both will.'

THE SUICIDE'S SPEARMAN

A family of the name of Spearman has lived in Cornwall for many ages, their native centre having been somewhere between Ludgvan and St Ives.

Years long ago, an unfortunate man, weary of life, destroyed himself; and the rude laws of a remote age, carrying out, as they thought, human punishments even after death, decreed that the body should be buried at the four cross-roads, and quicklime poured on the corpse.

Superstition stepped in and somewhat changed the order of burial. To prevent the dead man from 'walking', and becoming a terror to all his neighbours, the coffin was to be turned upside down, and a spear was to be driven through it and the body, so as to pin it to the ground.

It was with some difficulty that a man could be found to perform this task. At length, however, a blacksmith undertook it. He made the spear; and after the coffin was properly placed, he drove his spear-headed iron bar through it. From that day he was called 'the spearman', and his descendants have never lost the name.

In making a new road not many years since, the coffin and spear were found, and removed. From that time several old men and women have declared that the self-murderer 'walks the earth'.

ROBERT HUNT

THE BIRDS

DAPHNE DU MAURIER

On December the third the wind changed overnight and it was winter. Until then the autumn had been mellow, soft. The earth was rich where the plough had turned it.

Nat Hocken, because of a wartime disability, had a pension and did not work full-time at the farm. He worked three days a week, and they gave him the lighter jobs. Although he was married, with children, his was a solitary disposition; he liked best to work alone.

It pleased him when he was given a bank to build up, or a gate to mend, at the far end of the peninsula, where the sea surrounded the farmland on either side. Then, at midday, he would pause and eat the meat pie his wife had baked for him and, sitting on the cliff's edge, watch the birds.

In autumn great flocks of them came to the peninsula, restless, uneasy, spending themselves in motion; now wheeling, circling in the sky; now settling to feed on the rich, new-turned soil, but even when they fed, it was as though they did so without hunger, without desire.

Restlessness drove them to the skies again. Crying, whistling, calling, they skimmed the placid sea and left the shore.

Make haste, make speed, hurry and begone; yet where, and to what purpose? The restless urge of autumn, unsatisfying, sad, had put a spell upon them, and they must spill themselves of motion before winter came.

Perhaps, thought Nat, a message comes to the birds in autumn, like a warning. Winter is coming. Many of them will perish. And like people who, apprehensive of death before their time, drive themselves to work or folly, the birds do likewise; tomorrow we shall die.

The birds had been more restless than ever this fall of the year. Their agitation more remarked because the days were still.

As Mr Trigg's tractor traced its path up and down the western hills, and Nat, hedging, saw it dip and turn, the whole machine and the man upon it were momentarily lost in the great cloud of wheeling, crying birds.

Nat remarked upon them to Mr Trigg when the work was finished for the day.

'Yes,' said the farmer, 'there are more birds about than usual. I have a notion the weather will change. It will be a hard winter. That's why the birds are restless.'

The farmer was right. That night the weather turned.

The bedroom in the cottage faced east. Nat woke just after two and heard the east wind, cold and dry. It sounded hollow in the chimney, and a loose slate rattled on the roof. Nat listened, and he could hear the sea roaring in the bay. He drew the blanket round him, leaned closer to the back of his wife, deep in sleep. Then he heard the tapping on the window-pane. It continued until, irritated by the sound, Nat got out of bed and went to the window. He opened it; and as he did so something brushed his hand, jabbing at his knuckles, grazing the skin. Then he saw the flutter of wings and the thing was gone again, over the roof, behind the cottage.

It was a bird. What kind of bird he could not tell. The wind must have driven it to shelter on the sill.

He shut the window and went back to bed, but feeling his knuckles wet, put his mouth to the scratch. The bird had drawn blood.

Frightened, he supposed, bewildered, seeking shelter, the bird had stabbed at him in the darkness. Once more he settled himself to sleep.

Presently the tapping came again—this time more forceful, more insistent. And now his wife woke at the sound, and turning in the bed, said to him, 'See to the window, Nat; it's rattling.'

'I've already been to it,' he told her. 'There's some bird there, trying to get in.'

'Send it away,' she said. 'I can't sleep with that noise.'

He went to the window for the second time, and now when he opened it, there was not one bird on the sill but half a dozen; they flew straight into his face.

He shouted, striking out at them with his arms, scattering them; like the first one, they flew over the roof and disappeared.

He let the window fall and latched it.

Suddenly a frightened cry came from the room across the passage where the children slept.

'It's Jill,' said his wife, roused at the sound.

There came a second cry, this time from both children. Stumbling into their room, Nat felt the beating of wings about him in the darkness. The window was wide open. Through it came the birds, hitting first the ceiling and the walls, then swerving in mid-flight and turning to the children in their beds.

'It's all right. I'm here,' shouted Nat, and the children flung themselves, screaming, upon him, while in the darkness the birds rose, and dived, and came for him again.

'What is it, Nat? What's happened?' his wife called. Swiftly he pushed the children through the door to the passage and shut it upon them, so that he was alone in their bedroom with the birds.

He seized a blanket from the nearest bed, and using it as a weapon, flung it right and left about him.

He felt the thud of bodies, heard the fluttering of wings; but the birds were not yet defeated, for again and again they returned to the assault, jabbing his hands, his head, their little stabbing beaks sharp as pointed forks.

The blanket became a weapon of defence. He wound it about his head, and then in greater darkness, beat at the birds with his bare hands. He dared not stumble to the door and open it lest the birds follow him.

How long he fought with them in the darkness he could not tell; but at last the beating of the wings about him lessened, withdrew; and through the dense blanket he was aware of light.

He waited, listened; there was no sound except the fretful crying of one of the children from the bedroom beyond.

He took the blanket from his head and stared about him. The cold grey morning light exposed the room.

Dawn and the open window had called the living birds; the dead lay on the floor.

Sickened, Nat went to the window and stared out across his patch of garden to the fields.

It was bitter cold, and the ground had all the hard, black look of the frost that the east wind brings. The sea, fiercer now with turning tide, whitecapped and steep, broke harshly in the bay. Of the birds there was no sign.

Nat shut the window and door of the small bedroom and went back across the passage to his own room.

His wife sat up in bed, one child asleep beside her; the smaller one in her arms, his face bandaged.

'He's sleeping now,' she whispered. 'Something must have cut him; there was blood at the corners of his eyes. Jill said it was the birds. She said she woke up and the birds were in the room.'

His wife looked up at Nat, searching his face for confirmation. She looked terrified, bewildered. He did not want her to know that he also was shaken, dazed almost, by the events of the past few hours.

'There are birds in there,' he said. 'Dead birds, nearly fifty of them.'

He sat down on the bed beside his wife.

'It's the hard weather,' he said. 'It must be that; it's the hard weather. They aren't the birds, maybe, from around here. They've been driven down from up-country.'

'But Nat,' whispered his wife, 'it's only this night that the weather turned. They can't be hungry yet. There's food for them out there in the fields.'

'It's the weather,' repeated Nat. 'I tell you, it's the weather.

His face, too, was drawn and tired, like hers. They stared at one another for a while without speaking.

Nat went to the window and looked out. The sky was hard and leaden, and the brown hills that had gleamed in the sun the day before looked dark and bare. Black winter had descended in a single night.

The children were awake now. Jill was chattering, and young Johnny was crying once again. Nat heard his wife's voice, soothing, comforting them as he went downstairs.

Presently they came down. He had breakfast ready for them.

'Did you drive away the birds?' asked Jill.

'Yes, they've all gone now,' Nat said. 'It was the east wind brought them in.'

'I hope they won't come again,' said Jill.

'I'll walk with you to the bus,' Nat said to her.

Jill seemed to have forgotten her experience of the night before. She danced ahead of him, chasing the leaves, her face rosy under her pixy hood.

All the while Nat searched the hedgerows for the birds, glanced over them to the fields beyond, looked to the small wood above the farm where the rooks and jackdaws gathered; he saw none. Soon the bus came ambling up the hill.

Nat saw Jill on to the bus, then turned and walked back towards the farm. It was not his day for work, but he wanted to satisfy himself that all was well. He went to the back door of the farmhouse; he heard Mrs Trigg singing, the wireless making a background for her song.

'Are you there, missus?' Nat called.

She came to the door, beaming, broad, a good-tempered woman.

'Hullo, Mr Hocken,' she said. 'Can you tell me where this cold is coming from? Is it Russia? I've never seen such a change. And it's going on, the wireless says. Something to do with the Arctic Circle.'

'We didn't turn on the wireless this morning,' said Nat. 'Fact is, we had trouble in the night.'

'Kiddies poorly?'

'No.' He hardly knew how to explain. Now, in daylight, the battle of the birds would sound absurd.

He tried to tell Mrs Trigg what had happened, but he could see from her eyes that she thought his story was the result of nightmare following a heavy meal.

'Sure they were real birds?' she said, smiling.

'Mrs Trigg,' he said, 'there are fifty dead birds—robins, wrens, went for me; they tried to go for young Johnny's eyes.'

Mrs Trigg stared at him doubtfully. 'Well, now,' she answered. 'I suppose the weather brought them; once in the bedroom they wouldn't know where they were. Foreign birds maybe, from that Arctic Circle.'

'No,' said Nat. 'They were birds you see about here every day.'

'Funny thing,' said Mrs Trigg. 'No explaining it, really. You ought to write up and ask the *Guardian*. They'd have some answer for it. Well, I must be getting on.'

Nat walked back along the lane to his cottage. He found his wife in the kitchen with young Johnny.

'See anyone?' she asked.

'Mrs Trigg,' he answered. 'I don't think she believed me. Anyway, nothing wrong up there.'

'You might take the birds away,' she said. 'I daren't go into the room to make the beds until you do. I'm scared.'

'Nothing to scare you now,' said Nat. 'They're dead, aren't they?'

He went up with a sack and dropped the stiff bodies into it, one by one. Yes, there were fifty of them all told. Just the ordinary, common birds of the hedgerow; nothing as large even as a thrush. It must have been fright that made them act the way they did.

He took the sack out into the garden and was faced with a fresh problem. The ground was frozen solid, yet no snow had fallen; nothing had happened in the past hours but the coming of the east wind. It was unnatural, queer. He could see the whitecapped seas breaking in the bay. He decided to take the birds to the shore and bury them.

When he reached the beach below the headland, he could scarcely stand, the force of the east wind was so strong. It was low tide; he crunched his way over the shingle to the softer sand and then, his back to the wind, opened up his sack.

He ground a pit in the sand with his heel, meaning to drop the birds into it; but as he did so, the force of the wind lifted them as though in flight again, and they were blown away from him along the beach, tossed like feathers, spread and scattered.

The tide will take them when it turns, he said to himself.

He looked out to sea and watched the crested breakers, combing green. They rose stiffly, curled, and broke again; and because it was ebb tide, the roar was distant, more remote, lacking the sound and thunder of the flood.

Then he saw them. The gulls. Out there, riding the seas.

What he had thought at first were the whitecaps of the waves were gulls. Hundreds, thousands, tens of thousands.

They rose and fell in the troughs of the seas, heads to the wind, like a mighty fleet at anchor, waiting on the tide.

Nat turned; leaving the beach, he climbed the steep path home.

Someone should know of this. Someone should be told. Something was happening, because of the east wind and the weather, that he did not understand.

As he drew near the cottage, his wife came to meet him at the door. She called to him, excited. 'Nat,' she said, 'it's on the wireless. They've just read out a special news bulletin. It's not only here, it's everywhere. In London, all over the country. Something has happened to the birds. Come and listen; they're repeating it.'

Together they went into the kitchen to listen to the announcement.

'Statement from the Home Office, at eleven am this morning. Reports from all over the country are coming in hourly about the vast quantity of birds flocking above towns, villages, and outlying districts, causing obstruction and damage and even attacking individuals. It is thought that the Arctic air stream at present covering the British Isles is causing birds to migrate south in immense numbers, and that intense hunger may drive these birds to attack human beings. Householders are warned to see to their windows, doors and chimneys, and to take reasonable precautions for the safety of their children. A further statement will be issued later.'

A kind of excitement seized Nat. He looked at his wife in triumph. 'There you are,' he said. 'I've been telling myself all morning there's something wrong. And just now, down on the beach, I looked out to sea and there were gulls, thousands of them, riding on the sea, waiting.'

'What are they waiting for, Nat?' she asked.

He stared at her. 'I don't know,' he said slowly.

He went over to the drawer where he kept his hammer and other tools.

'What are you going to do, Nat?'

'See to the windows and the chimneys, like they tell you to.'

'You think they would break in with the windows shut? Those wrens and robins and such? Why, how could they?'

He did not answer. He was not thinking of the robins and the wrens. He was thinking of the gulls.

He went upstairs and worked there the rest of the morning, boarding the windows of the bedrooms, filling up the chimney bases.

'Dinner's ready.' His wife called him from the kitchen.

'All right. Coming down.'

When dinner was over and his wife was washing up, Nat switched on the one o'clock news. The same announcement was repeated, but the news bulletin enlarged upon it. 'The flocks of birds have caused dislocation in all areas,' said the announcer, 'and in London the mass was so dense at ten o'clock this morning that it seemed like a vast black cloud. The birds settled on rooftops, on window ledges, and on chimneys. The species included blackbird, thrush, the common house sparrow, and as might be expected in the metropolis, a vast quantity of pigeons, starlings, and that frequenter of the London river, the black-headed gull. The sight was so unusual that traffic came to a standstill in many thoroughfares, work was abandoned in shops and offices, and the streets and pavements were crowded with people standing about to watch the birds.'

The announcer's voice was smooth and suave; Nat had the impression that he treated the whole business as he would an elaborate joke. There would be others like him, hundreds of them, who did not know what it was to struggle in darkness with a flock of birds.

Nat switched off the wireless. He got up and started work on the kitchen windows. His wife watched him, young Johnny at her heels.

'What they ought to do,' she said, 'is to call the Army out and shoot the birds.'

'Let them try,' said Nat. 'How'd they set about it?'

'I don't know. But something should be done. They ought to do something.'

Nat thought to himself that 'they' were no doubt considering the problem at that very moment, but whatever 'they' decided to do in London and the big cities would not help them here, nearly three hundred miles away.

'How are we off for food?' he asked.

'It's shopping day tomorrow, you know that. I don't keep uncooked food about. Butcher doesn't call till the day after. But I can bring back something when I go in tomorrow.'

Nat did not want to scare her. He looked in the larder for himself and in the cupboard where she kept her tins.

They could hold out for a couple of days.

He went on hammering the boards across the kitchen windows. Candles. They were low on candles. That must be another thing she meant to buy tomorrow. Well, they must go early to bed tonight. That was, if—

He got up and went out the back door and stood in the garden, looking down towards the sea.

There had been no sun all day, and now at barely three o'clock, a kind of darkness had already come; the sky was sullen, heavy, colourless like salt. He could hear the vicious sea drumming on the rocks.

He walked down the path halfway to the beach. And then he stopped. He could see the tide had turned. The gulls had risen. They were circling, hundreds of them, thousands of them, lifting their wings against the wind.

It was the gulls that made the darkening of the sky.

And they were silent. They just went on soaring and circling, rising, falling, trying their strength against the wind. Nat turned. He ran up the path back to the cottage.

'I'm going for Jill,' he said to his wife.

'What's the matter?' she asked. 'You've gone quite white.'

'Keep Johnny inside,' he said. 'Keep the door shut. Light up now and draw the curtains.'

'It's only gone three,' she said.

'Never mind. Do what I tell you.'

He looked inside the tool shed and took the hoe.

He started walking up the lane to the bus stop. Now and again he glanced back over his shoulder; and he could see the gulls had risen higher now, their circles were broader, they were spreading out in huge formation across the sky.

He hurried on. Although he knew the bus would not come before four o'clock, he had to hurry.

He waited at the top of the hill. There was half an hour still to go.

The east wind came whipping across the fields from the higher ground. In the distance he could see the clay hills, white and clean against the heavy pallor of the sky.

Something black rose from behind them, like a smudge at first, then widening, becoming deeper. The smudge became a cloud; and the cloud divided again into five other clouds, spreading north, east, south, and west; and then they were not clouds at all but birds.

He watched them travel across the sky, within two or three hundred feet of him. He knew, from their speed, that they were bound inland; they had no business with the people here on the peninsula. They were rooks, crows, jackdaws, magpies, jays, all birds that usually preyed upon the small species, but bound this afternoon on some other mission.

He went to the telephone call box, stepped inside, lifted the receiver. The exchange would pass the message on. 'I'm speaking from the highway,' he said, 'by the bus stop. I want to report large formations of birds travelling up-country. The gulls are also forming in the bay.'

'All right,' answered the voice, laconic, weary.

'You'll be sure and pass this message on to the proper quarter?'

'Yes. Yes.' Impatient now, fed up. The buzzing note resumed. She's another, thought Nat. She doesn't care.

The bus came lumbering up the hill. Jill climbed out.

'What's the hoe for, Dad?'

'I just brought it along,' he said. 'Come on now, let's get home. It's cold; no hanging about. See how fast you can run.'

He could see the gulls now, still silent, circling the fields, coming in towards the land.

'Look, Dad; look over there. Look at all the gulls.'

'Yes. Hurry now.'

'Where are they flying? Where are they going?'

'Up-country, I dare say. Where it's warmer.'

He seized her hand and dragged her after him along the lane.

'Don't go so fast. I can't keep up.'

The gulls were copying the rooks and crows. They were spreading out, in formation, across the sky. They headed, in bands of thousands, to the four compass points.

'Dad, what is it? What are the gulls doing?'

They were not intent upon their flight, as the crows, as the jackdaws, had been. They still circled overhead. Nor did they fly so high. It was as though they waited upon some signal; as though some decision had yet to be given.

'I wish the gulls would go away.' Jill was crying. 'I don't like them. They're coming closer to the lane.'

He started running, swinging Jill after him. As they went past the farm turning, he saw the farmer backing his car into the garage. Nat called to him.

'Can you give us a lift?' he said.

Mr Trigg turned in the driver's seat and stared at them. Then a smile came to his cheerful, rubicund face. 'It looks as though we're in for some fun,' he said. 'Have you seen the gulls? Jim and I are going to take a crack at them. Everyone's gone bird crazy, talking of nothing else. I hear you were troubled in the night. Want a gun?'

Nat shook his head.

The small car was packed, but there was room for Jill on the back seat.

'I don't want a gun,' said Nat, 'but I'd be obliged if you'd run Jill home. She's scared of the birds.'

'Okay,' said the farmer. 'I'll take her home. Why don't you stop behind and join in the shooting-match? We'll make the feathers fly.'

Jill climbed in, and turning the car, the driver sped up the lane. Nat followed after. Trigg must be crazy. What use was a gun against a sky of birds?

They were coming in now towards the farm, circling lower in the sky. The farm, then, was their target. Nat increased his pace towards his own cottage. He saw the farmer's car turn and come back along the lane. It drew up beside him with a jerk.

'The kid has run inside,' said the farmer. 'Your wife was watching for her. Well, what do you make of it? They're saying in town the Russians have done it. The Russians have poisoned the birds.'

'How could they do that?' asked Nat.

'Don't ask me. You know how stories get around.'

'Have you boarded your windows?' asked Nat.

'No. Lot of nonsense. I've had more to do today than to go round boarding up my windows.'

'I'd board them now if I were you.'

'Garn. You're windy. Like to come to our place to sleep?'

'No, thanks all the same.'

'All right. See you in the morning. Give you a gull breakfast.'

The farmer grinned and turned his car to the farm entrance. Nat hurried on. Past the little wood, past the old barn, and then across the stile to the remaining field. As he jumped the stile, he heard the whir of wings. A black-backed gull dived down at him from the sky. It missed, swerved in flight, and rose to dive again. In a moment it was joined by others—six, seven, a dozen.

Nat dropped his hoe. The hoe was useless. Covering his head with his arms, he ran towards the cottage.

They kept coming at him from the air—noiseless, silent, save for the beating wings. The terrible, fluttering wings. He could feel the blood on his hands, his wrists, upon his neck. If only he could keep them from his eyes. Nothing else mattered.

With each dive, with each attack, they became bolder. And they had no thought for themselves. When they dived low and missed, they crashed, bruised and broken on the ground.

As Nat ran he stumbled, kicking their spent bodies in front of him.

He found the door and hammered upon it with bleeding hands. 'Let me in,' he shouted. 'It's Nat. Let me in.'

Then he saw the gannet, poised for the dive, above him in the sky.

The gulls circled, retired, soared, one with another, against the wind.

Only the gannet remained. One single gannet, above him in the sky. Its wings folded suddenly to its body. It dropped like a stone.

Nat screamed; and the door opened.

He stumbled across the threshold, and his wife threw her weight against the door.

They heard the thud of the gannet as it fell.

His wife dressed his wounds. They were not deep. The backs of his hands had suffered most, and his wrists. Had he not worn a cap, the birds would have reached his head. As for the gannet—the gannet could have split his skull.

The children were crying, of course. They had seen the blood on their father's hands.

'It's all right now,' he told them. 'I'm not hurt.'

His wife was ashen. 'I saw them overhead,' she whispered. 'They began collecting just as Jill ran in with Mr Trigg. I shut the door fast, and it jammed. That's why I couldn't open it at once when you came.'

'Thank God the birds waited for me,' he said. 'Jill would have fallen at once. They're flying inland, thousands of them. Rooks, crows, all the bigger birds. I saw them from the bus stop. They're making for the towns.'

'But what can they do, Nat?'

'They'll attack. Go for everyone out in the streets. Then they'll try the windows, the chimneys.'

'Why don't the authorities do something? Why don't they get the Army, get machine guns?'

'There's been no time. Nobody's prepared. We'll hear what they have to say on the six o'clock news.'

'I can hear the birds,' Jill said. 'Listen, Dad.'

Nat listened. Muffled sounds came from the windows, from the door. Wings brushing the surface, sliding, scraping, seeking a way of entry. The sound of many bodies pressed together, shuffling on the sills. Now and again came a thud, a crash, as some bird dived and fell.

Some of them will kill themselves that way, he thought, but not enough. Never enough.

'All right,' he said aloud. 'I've got boards over the windows, Jill. The birds can't get in.'

He went and examined all the windows. He found wedges —pieces of old tin, strips of wood and metal—and fastened them at the sides of the windows to reinforce the boards.

His hammerings helped to deafen the sound of the birds, the shuffling, the tapping, and—more ominous—the splinter of breaking glass.

'Turn on the wireless,' he said.

He went upstairs to the bedrooms and reinforced the windows there. Now he could hear the birds on the roof—the scraping of claws, a sliding, jostling sound.

He decided the whole family must sleep in the kitchen and keep up the fire. He was afraid of the bedroom chimneys. The boards he had placed at their bases might give way. In the kitchen they would be safe because of the fire.

He would have to make a joke of it. Pretend to the children they were playing camp. If the worst happened and the birds forced an entry by way of the bedroom chimneys, it would be hours, days perhaps, before they could break down the doors. The birds would be imprisoned in the bedrooms. They could do no harm there. Crowded together, they would stifle and die. He began to bring the mattresses downstairs.

At sight of them, his wife's eyes widened in apprehension. 'All right,' he said cheerfully. 'We'll all sleep together in the kitchen tonight. More cosy, here by the fire. Then we won't be worried by those silly old birds tapping at the windows.'

He made the children help him rearrange the furniture, and he took the precaution of moving the dresser against the windows.

We're safe enough now, he thought. We're snug and tight. We can hold out. It's just the food that worries me. Food and coal for the fire. We've enough for two or three days, not more. By that time—

No use thinking ahead as far as that. And they'd be given directions on the wireless.

And now, in the midst of many problems, he realized that only dance music was coming over the air. He knew the reason. The usual programmes had been abandoned; this only happened at exceptional times.

At six o'clock the records ceased. The time signal was given. There was a pause, and then the announcer spoke. His voice was solemn, grave. Quite different from midday.

'This is London,' he said. 'A national emergency was proclaimed at four o'clock this afternoon. Measures are being taken to safeguard the lives and property of the population, but it must be understood that these are not easy to effect immediately, owing to the unforeseen and unparalleled nature of the present crisis. Every householder must take precautions about his own building. Where several people live together, as in flats and hotels, they must unite to do the utmost that they can to prevent entry. It is absolutely imperative that every individual stay indoors tonight.

'The birds, in vast numbers, are attacking anyone on sight, and have already begun an assault upon buildings; but these, with due care, should be impenetrable.

'The population is asked to remain calm.

'Owing to the exceptional nature of the emergency, there will be no further transmission from any broadcasting station until seven am tomorrow.'

They played 'God Save the Queen'. Nothing more happened.

Nat switched off the set. He looked at his wife. She stared back at him.

'We'll have supper early,' suggested Nat. 'Something for a treat—toasted cheese, eh? Something we all like.'

He winked and nodded at his wife. He wanted the look of dread, of apprehension, to leave her face.

He helped with the supper, whistling, singing, making as much clatter as he could. It seemed to him that the shuffling and the tapping were not so intense as they had been at first, and presently he went up to the bedrooms and listened. He no longer heard the jostling for place upon the roof.

They've got reasoning powers, he thought. They know it's hard to break in here. They'll try elsewhere.

Supper passed without incident. Then, when they were clearing away, they heard a new sound, a familiar droning.

His wife looked up at him, her face alight.

'It's planes,' she said. 'They're sending out planes after the birds. That will get them. Isn't that gunfire? Can't you hear guns?'

It might be gunfire, out at sea. Nat could not tell. Big naval guns might have some effect upon the gulls out at sea, but the gulls were inland now. The guns couldn't shell the shore because of the population.

'It's good, isn't it,' said his wife, 'to hear the planes?'

Catching her enthusiasm, Jill jumped up and down with Johnny. 'The planes will get the birds.'

Just then they heard a crash about two miles distant. Followed by a second, then a third. The droning became more distant, passed away out to sea.

'What was that?' asked his wife.

'I don't know,' answered Nat. He did not want to tell her that the sound they had heard was the crashing of aircraft.

It was, he had no doubt, a gamble on the part of the authorities to send out reconnaissance forces, but they might have known the gamble was suicidal. What could aircraft do against birds that flung themselves to death against propeller and fuselage but hurtle to the ground themselves?

'Where have the planes gone, Dad?' asked Jill.

'Back to base,' he said. 'Come on now, time to tuck down for bed.'

There was no further drone of aircraft, and the naval guns had ceased. Waste of life and effort, Nat said to himself. We can't destroy enough of them that way. Cost too heavy. There's always gas. Maybe they'll try spraying with gas, mustard gas. We'll be warned first, of course, if they do. There's one thing, the best brains of the country will be on it tonight.

Upstairs in the bedrooms all was quiet. No more scraping and stabbing at the windows. A lull in battle. The wind hadn't dropped, though. Nat could still hear it roaring in the chimneys. And the sea breaking down on the shore.

Then he remembered the tide. The tide would be on the turn. Maybe the lull in battle was because of the tide. There was some law the birds obeyed, and it had to do with the east wind and the tide.

He glanced at his watch. Nearly eight o'clock. It must have gone high water an hour ago. That explained the lull. The birds attacked with the flood tide.

He reckoned the time limit in his head. They had six hours to go without attack. When the tide turned again, around 1.20 in the morning, the birds would come back.

He called softly to his wife and whispered to her that he would go out and see how they were faring at the farm, see if the telephone was still working there so that they might get news from the exchange.

'You're not to go,' she said at once, 'and leave me alone with the children. I can't stand it.'

'All right,' he said, 'all right. I'll wait till morning. And we can get the wireless bulletin then, too, at seven. But when the tide ebbs again, I'll try for the farm; they may let us have bread and potatoes.'

His mind was busy again, planning against emergency. They would not have milked, of course, this evening. The cows would be standing by the gate, waiting; the household would be inside, battened behind boards as they were here at the cottage.

That is, if they had had time to take precautions.

Softly, stealthily, he opened the back door and looked outside.

It was pitch-dark. The wind was blowing harder than ever, coming in steady gusts, icy, from the sea.

He kicked at the step. It was heaped with birds. These were the suicides, the divers, the ones with broken necks. Wherever he looked, he saw dead birds. The living had flown seaward with the turn of the tide. The gulls would be riding the seas now, as they had done in the forenoon.

In the far distance on the hill, something was burning. One of the aircraft that had crashed; the fire, fanned by the wind, had set light to a stack.

He looked at the bodies of the birds. He had a notion that if he stacked them, one upon the other, on the window sills, they would be added protection against the next attack.

Not much, perhaps, but something. The bodies would have to be clawed at, pecked and dragged aside before the living birds gained purchase on the sills and attacked the panes.

He set to work in the darkness. It was queer. He hated touching the dead birds, but he went on with his work. He noticed grimly that every window-pane was shattered. Only the boards had kept the birds from breaking in.

He stuffed the cracked pains with the bleeding bodies of the birds and felt his stomach turn. When he had finished, he went back into the cottage and barricaded the kitchen door, making it doubly secure.

His wife had made him cocoa; he drank it thirstily. He was very tired. 'All right,' he said, smiling, 'don't worry. We'll get through.'

He lay down on his mattress and closed his eyes.

He dreamed uneasily because, through his dreams, ran the dread of something forgotten. Some piece of work that he should have done. It was connected, in some way, with the burning aircraft.

It was his wife, shaking his shoulder, who awoke him finally.

'They've begun,' she sobbed. 'They've started this last hour. I can't listen to it any longer alone. There's something smells bad too, something burning.'

Then he remembered. He had forgotten to make up the fire.

The fire was smouldering, nearly out. He got up swiftly and lighted the lamp.

The hammering had started at the windows and the door, but it was not that he minded now. It was the smell of singed feathers.

The smell filled the kitchen. He knew what it was at once. The birds were coming down the chimney, squeezing their way down to the kitchen range.

He got sticks and paper and put them on the embers, then reached for the can of kerosene.

'Stand back,' he shouted to his wife. He threw some of the kerosene on to the fire.

The flame roared up the pipe, and down into the fire fell the scorched, blackened bodies of the birds.

The children waked, crying. 'What is it?' asked Jill. 'What's happened?'

Nat had no time to answer her. He was raking the bodies from the chimney, clawing them out on to the floor.

The flames would drive away the living birds from the chimney top. The lower joint was the difficulty though. It was choked with the smouldering, helpless bodies of the birds caught by fire.

He scarcely heeded the attack on the windows and the door. Let them beat their wings, break their backs, lose their lives, in the desperate attempt to force an entry into his home. They would not break in.

'Stop crying,' he called to the children. 'There's nothing to be afraid of. Stop crying.'

He went on raking out the burning, smouldering bodies as they fell into the fire.

This'll fetch them, he said to himself. The draught and the flames together. We're all right as long as the chimney doesn't catch.

Amid the tearing at the window boards came the sudden homely striking of the kitchen clock. Three o'clock.

A little more than four hours to go. He could not be sure of the exact time of high water. He reckoned the tide would not turn much before half-past seven.

He waited by the range. The flames were dying. But no more blackened bodies fell from the chimney. He thrust his poker up as far as it could go and found nothing.

The danger of the chimney's being choked up was over. It could not happen again, not if the fire was kept burning day and night.

I'll have to get more fuel from the farm tomorrow, he thought. I can do all that with the ebb tide. It can be worked; we can fetch what we need when the tide's turned. We've just got to adapt ourselves, that's all.

They drank tea and cocoa, ate slices of bread. Only half a loaf left, Nat noticed. Never mind, though; they'd get by.

If they could hang on like this until seven, when the first news bulletin came through, they would not have done too badly.

'Give us a smoke,' he said to his wife. 'It will clear away the smell of the scorched feathers.'

'There's only two left in the packet,' she said. 'I was going to buy you some.'

'I'll have one,' he said.

He sat with one arm around his wife and one around Jill, with Johnny on his lap, the blankets heaped about them on the mattress.

'You can't help admiring the beggars,' he said. 'They've got persistency. You'd think they'd tire of the game, but not a bit of it.'

Admiration was hard to sustain. The tapping went on and on; and a new, rasping note struck Nat's ear, as though a sharper beak than any hitherto had come to take over from its fellows.

He tried to remember the names of birds; he tried to think which species would go for this particular job.

It was not the tap of the woodpecker. That would be light and frequent. This was more serious; if it continued long, the wood would splinter as the glass had done.

Then he remembered the hawks. Could the hawks have taken over from the gulls? Were there buzzards now upon the sills, using talons as well as beaks? Hawks, buzzards, kestrels, falcons; he had forgotten the birds of prey. He had forgotten the gripping power of the birds of prey. Three hours to go; and while they waited, the sound of the splintering wood, the talons tearing at the wood.

Nat looked about him, seeing what furniture he could destroy to fortify the door.

The windows were safe because of the dresser. He was not certain of the door. He went upstairs; but when he reached the landing, he paused and listened.

There was a soft patter on the floor of the children's bedroom. The birds had broken through.

The other bedroom was still clear. He brought out the furniture to pile at the head of the stairs should the door of the children's bedroom go.

'Come down, Nat. What are you doing?' called his wife.

'I won't be long,' he shouted. 'I'm just making everything ship-shape up here.'

He did not want her to come. He did not want her to hear the pattering in the children's bedroom, the brushing of those wings against the door.

After he suggested breakfast, he found himself watching the clock, gazing at the hands that went so slowly around the dial. If his theory was not correct, if the attack did not cease with the turn of the tide, he knew they were beaten. They could not continue through the long day without air, without rest, without fuel.

A crackling in his ears drove away the sudden desperate desire for sleep.

'What is it? What now?' he said sharply.

'The wireless,' said his wife. 'I've been watching the clock. It's nearly seven.'

The comfortable crackling of the wireless brought new life.

They waited. The kitchen clock struck seven.

The crackling continued. Nothing else. No chimes. No music.

'We heard wrong,' he said. 'They won't be broadcasting until eight o'clock.'

They left the wireless switched on. Nat thought of the battery, wondered how much power was left in the battery. If it failed, they would not hear the instructions.

'It's getting light,' whispered his wife. 'I can't see it but I can feel it. And listen! The birds aren't hammering so loud now.'

She was right. The rasping, tearing sound grew fainter every moment. So did the shuffling, the jostling for place upon the step, upon the sills. The tide was on the turn.

By eight there was no sound at all. Only the wind. And the crackling of the wireless. The children, lulled at least by the stillness, fell asleep.

At half-past eight Nat switched the wireless off.

'We'll miss the news,' said his wife.

'There isn't going to be any news,' said Nat. 'We've got to depend upon ourselves.'

He went to the door and slowly pulled away the barricades. He drew the bolts, and kicking the broken bodies from the step outside the door, breathed the cold air.

He had six working hours before him, and he knew he must reserve his strength to the utmost, not waste it in any way.

Food and light and fuel; these were the most necessary things. If he could get them, they could endure another night.

He stepped into the garden; and as he did so, he saw the living birds. The gulls had gone to ride the sea, as they had done before. They sought sea food and the buoyancy of the tide before they returned to the attack.

Not so the land birds. They waited and watched.

Nat saw them on the hedgerows, on the soil, crowded in the trees, outside in the field—line upon line of birds, still, doing nothing. He went to the end of his small garden.

The birds did not move. They merely watched him.

I've got to get food, Nat said to himself. I've got to go to the farm to get food.

He went back to the cottage. He saw to the windows and the door.

'I'm going to the farm,' he said.

His wife clung to him. She had seen the living birds from the open door.

'Take us with you,' she begged. 'We can't stay here alone. I'd rather die than stay here alone.'

'Come on, then,' he said. 'Bring baskets and Johnny's pram. We can load up the pram.'

They dressed against the biting wind. His wife put Johnny in the pram, and Nat took Jill's hand.

'The birds,' Jill whimpered. 'They're all out there in the fields.'

'They won't hurt us,' he said. 'Not in the light.'

They started walking across the field towards the stile, and the birds did not move. They waited, their heads turned to the wind.

When they reached the turning to the farm, Nat stopped and told his wife to wait in the shelter of the hedge with the two children. 'But I want to see Mrs Trigg,' she protested. 'There are lots of things we can borrow if they went to market yesterday, and—'

'Wait here,' Nat interrupted. 'I'll be back in a moment.'

The cows were lowing, moving restlessly in the yard, and he could see a gap in the fence where the sheep had knocked their way through to roam unchecked in the front garden before the farmhouse.

No smoke came from the chimneys. Nat was filled with misgiving. He did not want his wife or the children to go down to the farm.

He went down alone, pushing his way through the herd of lowing cows, who turned this way and that, distressed, their udders full.

He saw the car standing by the gate. Not put away in the garage.

All the windows of the farmhouse were smashed. There were many dead gulls lying in the yard and around the house.

The living birds perched on the group of trees behind the farm and on the roof of the house. They were quite still. They watched him. Jim's body lay in the yard. What was left of it. His gun was beside him.

The door of the house was shut and bolted, but it was easy to push up a smashed window and climb through.

Trigg's body was close to the telephone. He must have

been trying to get through to the exchange when the birds got him. The receiver was off the hook, and the instrument was torn from the wall.

No sign of Mrs Trigg. She would be upstairs. Was it any use going up? Sickened, Nat knew what he would find there.

Thank God, he said to himself, there were no children.

He forced himself to climb the stairs, but halfway up he turned and descended again. He could see Mrs Trigg's legs protruding from the open bedroom door. Beside her were the bodies of black-backed gulls and an umbrella, broken. It's no use doing anything, Nat thought. I've only got five hours; less than that. The Triggs would understand. I must load up with what I can find.

He tramped back to his wife and children.

'I'm going to fill up the car with stuff,' he said. 'We'll take it home and return for a fresh load.'

'What about the Triggs?' asked his wife.

'They must have gone to friends,' he said.

'Shall I come and help you then?'

'No, there's a mess down there. Cows and sheep all over the place. Wait; I'll get the car. You can sit in the car.'

Her eyes watched his all the time he was talking. He believed she understood. Otherwise she certainly would have insisted on helping him find the bread and groceries.

They made three journeys altogether, to and from the farm, before he was satisfied they had everything they needed. It was surprising, once he started thinking, how many things were necessary. Almost the most important of all was planking for the windows. He had to go around searching for timber. He wanted to renew the boards on all the windows at the cottage.

On the final journey he drove the car to the bus stop and got out and went to the telephone box.

He waited a few minutes, jangling the hook. No good, though. The line was dead. He climbed on to a bank and looked over the countryside, but there was no sign of life at all, nothing in the fields but the waiting, watching birds.

Some of them slept; he could see their beaks tucked into their feathers.

You'd think they'd be feeding, he said to himself, not just standing that way.

Then he remembered. They were gorged with food. They had eaten their fill during the night. That was why they did not move this morning.

He lifted his face to the sky. It was colourless, grey. The bare trees looked bent and blackened by the east wind.

The cold did not affect the living birds, waiting out there in the fields.

This is the time they ought to get them, Nat said to himself. They're a sitting target now. They must be doing this all over the country. Why don't our aircraft take off now and spray them with mustard gas? What are all our chaps doing? They must know; they must see for themselves.

He went back to the car and got into the driver's seat.

'Go quickly past the second gate,' whispered his wife. 'The postman's lying there. I don't want Jill to see.'

It was a quarter to one by the time they reached the cottage. Only an hour to go.

'Better have dinner,' said Nat. 'Hot up something for yourself and the children, some of that soup. I've no time to eat now. I've got to unload all this stuff from the car.'

He got everything inside the cottage. It could be sorted later. Give them all something to do during the long hours ahead.

First he must see to the windows and the door.

He went around the cottage methodically, testing every window and the door. He climbed on to the roof also, and fixed boards across every chimney except the kitchen's.

The cold was so intense he could hardly bear it, but the job had to be done. Now and again he looked up, searching the sky for aircraft. None came. As he worked, he cursed the inefficiency of the authorities.

He paused, his work on the bedroom chimney finished, and looked out to sea. Something was moving out there. Something grey and white among the breakers.

'Good old Navy,' he said. 'They never let us down. They're coming down channel; they're turning into the bay.'

He waited, straining his eyes towards the sea. He was wrong, though. The Navy was not there. It was the gulls rising from the sea. And the massed flocks in the fields, with ruffled feathers, rose in formation from the ground and, wing to wing, soared upward to the sky.

The tide had turned again.

Nat climbed down the ladder and went inside the cottage. The family were at dinner. It was a little after two.

He bolted the door, put up the barricade, and lighted the lamp.

'It's night-time,' said young Johnny.

His wife had switched on the wireless once again. The crackling sound came, but nothing else.

'I've been all round the dial,' she said, 'foreign stations and all. I can't get anything but the crackling.'

'Maybe they have the same trouble,' he said. 'Maybe it's the same right through Europe.'

They ate in silence.

The tapping began at the windows, at the door, the rustling, the jostling, the pushing for position on the sills. The first thud of the suicide gulls upon the step.

When he had finished dinner, Nat planned, he would put the supplies away, stack them neatly, get everything shipshape. The boards were strong against the windows and across the chimneys. The cottage was filled with stores, with fuel, with all they needed for the next few days.

His wife could help him, and the children too. They'd tire themselves out between now and a quarter to nine, when the tide would ebb; then he'd tuck them down on their mattresses, see that they slept good and sound until three in the morning.

He had a new scheme for the windows, which was to fix barbed wire in front of the boards. He had brought a great roll of it from the farm. The nuisance was, he'd have to work at this in the dark, when the lull came between nine and three. Pity he had not thought of it before. Still, as long as the wife and kids slept—that was the main thing.

The smaller birds were at the windows now. He recognized the light tap-tapping of their beaks and the soft brush of their wings.

The hawks ignored the windows. They concentrated their attack upon the door.

Nat listened to the tearing sound of splintering wood, and wondered how many million years of memory were stored in those little brains, behind the stabbing beaks, the piercing eyes, now giving them this instinct to destroy mankind with all the deft precision of machines.

'I'll smoke that last cigarette,' he said to his wife. 'Stupid of me. It was the one thing I forgot to bring back from the farm.'

He reached for it, switched on the crackling wireless.

He threw the empty packet on to the fire and watched it burn.

THE BARGEST

Should you be out walking one evening in either a Cornish village, or among the hills, for heaven's sake keep your eyes open for a 'Bargest', or Spectre-Hound. It is a great brute, said to be the size of a full-grown bear, and the best advice that I can give is: make for the nearest river or stream, for it cannot cross water. Should there be no water handy, stand to one side, and let him 'have the wall', otherwise you may share the fate of a certain John Lambert, who was torn to pieces as a punishment for bad manners.

Needless to say, the appearance of a Bargest is said to precede a death.

R. C. H.

THE SPECTRE BRIDEGROOM

ROBERT HUNT

Long, long ago a farmer named Lenine lived in Boscean.

He had but one son, Frank Lenine, who was indulged into waywardness by both his parents. In addition to the farm servants, there was one, a young girl, Nancy Trenoweth, who especially assisted Mrs Lenine in all the various duties of a small farmhouse.

Nancy Trenoweth was very pretty, and although perfectly uneducated, in the sense in which we now employ the term education, she possessed many native graces, and she had acquired much knowledge, really useful to one whose aspirations would probably never rise higher than to be mistress of a farm of a few acres. Educated by parents who had certainly never seen the world beyond Penzance, her ideas of the world were limited to a few miles around the Land's End. But although her book of nature was a small one, it had deeply impressed her mind with its influences. The wild waste, the small but fertile valley, the rugged hills, with their crowns of cairns, the moors rich in the golden furze and the purple heath, the sea-beaten cliffs, and the silver sands, were the pages she had studied, under the guidance of a mother who conceived, in the sublimity of her ignorance, that everything in nature was the home of some spirit form. The soul of the girl was imbued with the deeply religious dye of her mother's mind, whose religion was only a sense of an unknown world immediately beyond our own. The elder Nancy Trenoweth exerted over the villagers around her considerable power. They did not exactly fear her. She was too free from evil for that; but they were conscious of a mental superiority, and yielded without complaining to her sway.

The result of this was, that the younger Nancy, although compelled to service, always exhibited some pride, from a feeling that her mother was a superior woman to any around her.

She never felt herself inferior to her master and mistress, yet she complained not of being in subjection to them. There were so many interesting features in the character of this young servant girl that she became in many respects like a daughter to her mistress. There was no broad line of division in those days, in even the manorial hall, between the lord and his domestics, and still less defined was the position of the employer and the employed in a small farmhouse. Consequent on this condition of things, Frank Lenine and Nancy were thrown as much together as if they had been brother and sister. Frank was rarely checked in anything by his over-fond parents, who were especially proud of their son, since he was regarded as the handsomest young man in the parish. Frank conceived a very warm attachment for Nancy, and she was not a little proud of her lover. Although it was evident to all the parish that Frank and Nancy were seriously devoted to each other, the young man's parents were blind to it, and were taken by surprise when one day Frank asked his father and mother to consent to his marrying Nancy.

The Lenines had allowed their son to have his own way from his youth up; and now, in a matter which brought into play the strongest of human feelings, they were angry because he refused to bend to their wills.

The old man felt it would be a degradation for a Lenine to marry a Trenoweth, and, in the most unreasoning manner, he resolved it should never be.

The first act was to send Nancy home to Alsia Mill, where her parents resided; the next was an imperious command to his son never again to see the girl.

The commands of the old are generally powerless upon the young where the affairs of the heart are concerned. So were they upon Frank. He, who was rarely seen of an evening beyond the garden of his father's cottage, was now as constantly absent from his home. The house, which was wont to be a pleasant one, was strangely altered. A gloom had fallen over all things; the father and son rarely met as friends—the mother and her boy had now a feeling of reserve. Often there were angry altercations between the father and son, and the mother felt she could not become the defender of her boy in his open acts of disobedience, his bold defiance of his parents' commands.

Rarely an evening passed that did not find Nancy and Frank together in some retired nook. The Holy Well was a favourite meeting-place, and here the most solemn vows were made. Locks of hair were exchanged; a wedding-ring, taken from the finger of a corpse, was broken, when they vowed that they would be united either dead or alive; and they even climbed at night the granite-pile at Treryn, and swore by the Logan Rock the same strong vow.

Time passed onward thus unhappily, and, as the result of the endeavours to quench out the passion by force, it grew stronger under the repressing power, and, like imprisoned steam, eventually burst through all restraint.

Nancy's parents discovered at length that moonlight meetings between two untrained, impulsive youths, had a natural result, and they were now doubly earnest in their endeavours to compel Frank to marry their daughter.

The elder Lenine could not be brought to consent to this, and he firmly resolved to remove his son entirely from what he considered the hateful influences of the Trenoweths. He resolved to go to Plymouth, to take his son with him, and, if possible, to send him away to sea, hoping thus to wean him from his folly, as he considered this love-madness. Frank, poor fellow, with the best intentions, was not capable of any sustained effort, and consequently he at length succumbed to his father; and, to escape his persecution, he entered a ship bound for India, and bade adieu to his native land.

Frank could not write, and this happened in days when letters could be forwarded only with extreme difficulty, consequently Nancy never heard from her lover.

A baby had been born into a troublesome world, and the infant became a real solace to the young mother. As the child grew, it became an especial favourite with its grandmother; the elder Nancy rejoiced over the little prattler, and forgot her cause of sorrow. Young Nancy lived for her child, and on the memory of its father. Subdued in spirit she was, but her affliction had given force to her character, and she had been heard to declare that wherever Frank might be she was ever present with him; whatever might be the temptations of the hour, that her influence was all-powerful over him for good. She felt that no distance could separate their souls, that no time could be long enough to destroy the bond between them.

A period of distress fell upon the Trenoweths, and it was necessary that Nancy should leave her home once more, and go again into service. Her mother took charge of the babe, and she found a situation in the village of Kimyall, in the parish of Paul. Nancy, like her mother, contrived by force of character to maintain an ascendancy amongst her companions. She had formed an acquaintance, which certainly never grew into friendship, with some of the daughters of the small farmers around. These girls were all full of the superstitions of the time and place.

The winter was coming on, and nearly three years had passed away since Frank Lenine left his country. As yet there was no sign. Nor father, nor mother, nor maiden had heard of him, and they all sorrowed over his absence. The Lenines desired to have Nancy's child, but the Trenoweths would not part with it. They went so far even as to endeavour to persuade Nancy to live again with them, but Nancy was not at all disposed to submit to their wishes.

It was Allhallows Eve, and two of Nancy's companions persuaded her—no very difficult task—to go with them and sow hemp-seed.

At midnight the three maidens stole out unperceived into Kimyall town-place to perform their incantation. Nancy was the first to sow, the others being less bold than she.

Boldly she advanced, saying, as she scattered the seed—

'Hemp-seed I sów thee,
Hemp-seed grow thee;
And he who will my true love be,
Come after me
And shaw thee.'

This was repeated three times, when, looking back over her left shoulder, she saw Lenine; but he looked so angry that she shrieked with fear, and broke the spell. One of the other girls, however, resolved now to make trial of the spell, and the result of her labours was the vision of a white coffin. Fear now fell on all, and they went home sorrowful, to spend each one a sleepless night.

November came with its storms, and during one terrific night a large vessel was thrown upon the rocks in Bernowhall Cliff, and, beaten by the impetuous waves, she was soon in pieces. Amongst the bodies of the crew washed ashore, nearly all of whom had perished, was Frank Lenine. He was not dead when found, but the only words he lived to speak were begging the people to send for Nancy Trenoweth, that he might make her his wife before he died.

Rapidly sinking, Frank was borne by his friends on a litter to Boscean, but he died as he reached the town-place. His parents, overwhelmed in their own sorrows, thought nothing of Nancy, and without her knowing that Lenine had returned, the poor fellow was laid in his last bed, in Burian Churchyard.

On the night of the funeral, Nancy went, as was her custom, to lock the door of the house, and as was her custom too, she looked out into the night. At this instant a horseman rode up in hot haste, called her by name, and hailed her in a voice that made her blood boil.

The voice was the voice of Lenine. She could never forget that; and the horse she now saw was her sweetheart's favourite colt, on which he had often ridden at night to Alsia.

The rider was imperfectly seen; but he looked very sorrowful, and deadly pale, still Nancy knew him to be Frank Lenine.

He told her that he had just arrived home, and that the first moment he was at liberty he had taken horse to fetch his loved one, and to make her his bride.

Nancy's excitement was so great that she was easily persuaded to spring on the horse behind him, that they might reach his home before the morning.

When she took Lenine's hand a cold shiver passed through her, and as she grasped his waist to secure herself in her seat, her arm became as stiff as ice. She lost all power of speech, and suffered deep fear, yet she knew not why. The moon had arisen, and now burst out in a full flood of light, through the heavy clouds which had obscured it. The horse pursued its journey with great rapidity, and whenever in weariness it slackened its speed, the peculiar voice of the rider aroused its drooping energies. Beyond this no word was spoken since Nancy had mounted behind her lover. They now came to Trove Bottom, where there was no bridge at that time; they dashed into the river. The moon shone full in their faces. Nancy looked into the stream, and saw that the rider was in a shroud and other grave-clothes. She now knew that she was being carried away by a spirit, yet she had no power to save herself; indeed, the inclination to do so did not exist.

On went the horse at a furious pace, until they came to the blacksmith's shop near Burian Church-town, when she knew by the light from the forge fire thrown across the road that the smith was still at his labours. She now recovered speech. 'Save me! save me! save me!' she cried with all her might. The smith sprang from the door of the smithy, with a red-hot iron in his hand, and as the horse rushed by, caught the woman's dress and pulled her to the ground. The spirit, however, also seized Nancy's dress in one hand, and his grasp was like that of a vice. The horse passed like the wind, and Nancy and the smith were pulled down as far as the old Almshouses, near the churchyard. Here the horse for a moment stopped. The smith seized that moment, and with his hot iron burned off the dress from the rider's hand, thus saving Nancy, more dead than alive; while the rider passed over the wall of the churchyard, and vanished on the grave in which Lenine had been laid but a few hours before.

The smith took Nancy into his shop, and he soon aroused some of his neighbours, who took the poor girl back to Alsia. Her parents laid her on her bed. She spoke no word, but to ask for her child, to request her mother to give up her child to Lenine's parents, and her desire to be buried in his grave. Before the morning light fell on the world, Nancy had breathed her last breath.

A horse was seen that night to pass through the Churchtown like a ball from a musket, and in the morning Lenine's colt was found dead in Bernowhall Cliff, covered with foam, its eyes forced from its head, and its swollen tongue hanging out of its mouth. On Lenine's grave was found the piece of Nancy's dress which was left in the spirit's hand when the smith burnt her from his grasp.

It is said that one or two of the sailors who survived the wreck related after the funeral, how, on the 30th of October, at night, Lenine was like one mad; they could scarcely keep him in the ship. He seemed more asleep than awake, and, after great excitement, he fell as if dead upon the deck, and lay so for hours. When he came to himself, he told them that he had been taken to the village of Kimyall, and that if he ever married the woman who had cast the spell, he would make her suffer the longest day she had to live for drawing his soul out of his body.

Poor Nancy was buried in Lenine's grave, and her companion in sowing hemp-seed, who saw the white coffin, slept beside her within the year.

KENIDZHEK WITCH

On the tract called the 'Gump', near Kenidzhek, is a beautiful well of clear water, not far from which was a miner's cot, in which dwelt two miners with their sister. They told her never to go to the well after daylight; they would fetch the water for her. However, on one Saturday night she had forgotten to get in a supply for the morrow, so she went off to the well. Passing by a gap in a broken-down hedge (called a *gurgo*) near the well, she saw an old woman sitting down, wrapped in a red shawl; she asked her what she did there at that time of night, but received no reply. She thought this rather strange, but plunged her pitcher in the well; when she drew it up, though a perfectly sound vessel, it contained no water; she tried again and again, and, though she saw the water rushing in at the mouth of the pitcher, it was sure to be empty when lifted out. She then became rather frightened; spoke again to the old woman, but receiving no answer, hastened away, and came in great alarm to her brothers. They told her that it was on account of this old woman they did not wish her to go to the well at night. What she saw was the ghost of old Moll, a witch who had been a great terror to the people in her lifetime, and had laid many fearful spells on them. They said they saw her sitting in the gap by the wall every night when going to bed.

ROBERT HUNT

THE BODMIN TERROR

R. CHETWYND-HAYES

'Your nerves are like piano wires,' the specialist had said, 'don't overstrain them. I don't want to frighten you, but any undue excitement, and snap . . . Understand?'

He had nodded.

'Get away, somewhere quiet, take it easy—take it very easy. Are you married?'

Again he had nodded.

'Explain the situation to your wife, make her understand you must have peace . . .'

He had smiled, and wondered how Lydia would face the possibility that he might go mad if she did not treat him kindly—let him have peace.

'I'll go on a motoring tour of Cornwall,' he stated simply.

The specialist had frowned: 'I'm not at all sure it would be wise for you to drive a car for a prolonged period.'

'There is peace in Cornwall,' he had said.

The car had broken down some time after they had driven through Launceston, and although Lydia had demanded she spend the night there, James had refused to consider the possibility.

'I want to reach Lizard,' he said quietly, 'we have rooms reserved, or have you forgotten?'

'I have forgotten nothing,' her forehead was creased into a bad-tempered frown, 'but I'm tired, and I thought you might be considerate for a change.'

The car selected a nice quiet spot, then, after a preliminary warning splutter, ceased to function. James got out, raised the bonnet, and looked hopefully at the silent engine.

'Well?' Lydia snapped.

'Not a peep.' James touched what he thought might be a sparking plug, found it was hot, then sucked his finger.

'Do something,' Lydia ordered.

'My dear girl,' he came round to the open window, 'I can drive a car, but I haven't a clue how it works. Every man to his trade. I'm an artist, not a mechanic.'

'I see,' her long pale face was now sullen, the beautiful blue eyes cold with contempt, 'and what are we supposed to do?'

'Well,' he climbed into the car and closed the door, 'as I see it, we have two alternatives. One, we can start walking, and hope we come across an inn, or better still a garage. Or, we can stay put and trust that sooner or later a car will come along that will tow us to Lizard. I'm inclined to favour the latter. As you can see, a nasty mist is coming up, and I don't fancy traipsing through that.'

'You mean,' Lydia's slim body was now rigid, and he knew, were he to touch her, she would recoil, 'you intend to sit here and do nothing?'

'One cannot do nothing,' he corrected gently, 'I will sit still, and bask in the warmth of your company.'

The girl's face, half-hidden by her long auburn hair, was a sulky white mask, and James knew she wanted him to argue, work himself into a rage; lash her with harsh words. He suddenly felt very tired, and watched the mist drift across the moor: a milk-white cloud that soon veiled the peaks of Roughtor and Brown Willie; then he reached for his cigarette case.

'Oh, for heaven's sake, don't smoke,' she turned on him savagely, 'it's stuffy enough in here.'

'Sorry.' He put the case away.

'Christ, but it's cold. Can't you turn the heater on, or something?'

He turned up the collar of his overcoat: 'It won't give us much heat, unless the engine is running.'

He flinched at the tone of her voice as she said bitingly: 'Of all the stupid fools. Touring Cornwall in November. I must have been mad when I allowed you to talk me into it.'

'I think it was the new fur coat that did the trick,' he murmured.

'Oh, shut up.'

He switched on the headlights, and the mist instantly became a coloured screen, a whirling mass of orange silk, and the artist rejoiced.

'Cornwall, land of legend!' he said.

'What!'

The exclamation was like a punch in the ribs, but he turned a smiling face.

'Cornwall, if we are to believe the historians was once bedevilled by piskies, ghosts, and giants. Particularly giants, big fellows, anything from twenty to sixty feet tall.'

'Childish rubbish,' she snuggled down into the folds of her fur coat, 'that would appeal to you. Sometimes, James, I think you're more child than man.'

The figure emerged through the mist very slowly. First, it was the merest suggestion of a shadow; then it took shape, and an old woman crept into the circle of light cast by the head-lamps. She was small, little more than child size, with rounded shoulders, and a grotesquely wrinkled face in which a pair of black eyes gleamed like polished buttons; a dirty grey shawl covered her head and was tied in a loose knot under her chin. A long black gown enveloped the tiny figure from neck to ankle, and James felt the short hairs on his neck rise, while he shuddered. Lydia clutched his arm, her bad humour gone.

'An old woman. There must be a house nearby. Hot soup, a fire . . .'

She reached for the door handle, but his voice made her pause.

'Wait.'

'What for?' She stared at him over one shoulder. 'I'm sitting here freezing, and that old hag can give me warmth.'

'I . . .' he studied the brown wrinkled face and the unblinking little eyes, 'I don't like the look of her.'

'Who cares,' Lydia was now struggling with the door handle. 'It's all the same to me if she's Dracula's grandmother. She must have a house and a fire.'

It was then that the old woman pushed a tiny clawlike hand through the folds of her cloak, and beckoned.

'Look, she wants us to go with her.' Lydia was still having trouble with the door handle. 'Blast this thing. Why the hell don't you buy a decent car?'

'Yes, I can see she wants us to go with her,' James stared at the figure through the windscreen, 'but why doesn't she come round to the window, not stand there beckoning?'

'She's probably half cracked.' Lydia had the door open now, and the freezing mist poured in. 'So what? She can still light a fire, even cook.'

Reluctantly, James opened his door and climbed out. The mist got into his lungs, and he coughed—a rasping spasm that shook his body—so that he was obliged to lean against the car. When he recovered, Lydia was addressing the old woman.

'The car has broken down, and we're simply freezing. Could you put us up for the night? My husband will pay.'

The little shrouded figure backed away, then, without saying a word, beckoned again.

Lydia whispered to James as he stood beside her: 'I think the old thing's dumb.'

'Lydia, I'm not happy about this. Let's go back to the car; the mist will clear shortly, and someone is bound to come along.'

'Really James, you make me sick.' She pulled the fur coat tighter around her slim form. 'If you're frightened of an old woman, go hide in the car.' She strode after the grotesque little figure that was already almost hidden by the mist, and James, with a resigned shrug, could only follow.

They left the road after some twenty paces, and began to stumble across thick tufts of grass. More than once they blundered into gorse bushes. Lydia's temper soon became ruffled.

'For God's sake don't walk so quickly!' she screamed after the dim figure, 'this is not a cross country race.' The old woman stopped and waited patiently until they caught up, then, after beckoning again, moved onwards.

'I'm sorry,' Lydia apologized in a low voice, 'you were right, we ought to have stayed in the car.'

'Too late now,' he remarked grimly, 'we'd never find our way back. Probably finish up in a bog.'

The light began to fade twenty minutes later, and the mist became even denser. Suddenly, the old woman stopped, assumed a crouching position, then fumbled in the folds of her gown. They heard a scratching sound, and presently she turned round holding an ancient candle lantern. James whistled his astonishment.

'Unless I'm greatly mistaken, that's an old stage coach lamp, and I'll swear she lit it with a tinder box.'

'How much farther?' Lydia was breathing heavily, and he could feel her tremble.

'I say,' he called out, 'how much farther? My wife is very tired.'

He was completely ignored; the little figure scurried onwards, and they often had to run to keep the jerking lantern in view.

'Must be deaf and dumb,' he growled, 'I can't understand

how an old wreck like that can keep up such a cracking pace.'

'It's the Cornish air.' Lydia made a gallant effort to smile.

'Whatever the reason, she's still going too fast for me.' He raised his voice and shouted: 'Please don't go so fast.'

The lantern continued to bob up and down, and he thought he heard a low laugh.

It must have been an hour later when Lydia collapsed; she stumbled and would have fallen, were it not for James's encircling arm. He lowered her gently to the ground, then roared after the fast-disappearing lantern: 'My wife's fainted. Come back, please come back.'

The tiny spark of light became still, then to his relief it grew larger, and presently the old woman bent over the prostrate girl, and allowed the light to illuminate the pale face.

The voice was harsh, an overgrown, rasping whisper, only it was unlike any sound made by vocal cords; rather like sand-paper rubbed across velvet.

'Tired. Cold. Carry.'

James tried to lift Lydia, but his lungs were seared by the ice-chilled mist, and what strength he possessed had been spent on that nightmare journey. The old woman made a sound that could well have been a laugh.

'Weak. Hold.'

She held out the candle lantern, and James's manhood demanded he protest.

'No really, I can manage.'

'Hold.'

The word was a command, and he obeyed, holding the lamp high, puzzled as to what this frail bundle of bones imagined she could do. As he watched, ready to intervene should any rough measures be attempted to rouse Lydia from her faint, his puzzlement gradually turned to astonishment, then to stark, unreasoning terror.

Two claws, it was impossible to call them hands, being merely skin-wrapped bone, slid out from the gown, and after bunching Lydia's coat into a thick roll, heaved. With one effortless movement, the girl was lifted up over the shrouded head, and slumped down upon the rounded shoulders. Then with one arm about the nylon-clad legs and the other encircling the white neck, the old woman broke into a smart trot, with the now terrified James doing his best to keep up.

There was a pain at the back of his neck, and thoughts flashed across his brain like tracer bullets fired from a machine gun. Fear, love and hate; each emotion flowed into the other and became one continuous stream of pain-racked flame.

Lydia was to blame for this nightmare. Her stupid, sudden selfishness had driven them from the security of the car, and now he was following a dried up little monster, with Lydia's white thighs jolting up and down. And he wanted peace . . .

He had almost reached the limit of his endurance, when the mist began to thin out, and he saw the hill. A wedge-shaped crag, dressed in heather and skirted by gorse bushes, and at last, the old woman slackened her pace. Without hesitation, she forced her way through the bushes, not pausing until the rock face was reached. She did something with her foot. A kick? James could not see. Then, to his amazement, a door swung open, revealing a candlelit room beyond. The old woman trotted in, and did not stop until she reached a narrow, blanket-covered bed. On this she dumped Lydia, rather like a greengrocer depositing a sack of potatoes, then rubbed what passed for her hands together, while viewing James, who so far had ventured only a few steps beyond the doorway, with ill-concealed contempt.

'Come. Shut door.'

He was in a cave—a natural one, he decided, possibly enlarged and improved by someone long ago. The granite walls were smooth save for what appeared to be chisel marks; a fireplace had been dug out of the left-hand wall, and this was complete with flue, for a peat and log fire blazed in an old-fashioned iron grate. Although the cave was free from smoke, there was an indefinable smell—a stench was perhaps a better word—part animal, part corruption, as though the old woman shared her accommodation with a pig, or, more likely, some carnivorous animal which had left its half-consumed dinner to grow ripe in a dark corner. At the same time an occasional savoury smell came from a cooking pot dangling on a hook over the fire, and gave a kind of fillip to the overall stench, making James wonder if he were not encountering the ghosts of many long dead meals.

Some kind of rush matting covered the floor. A sturdy, age-darkened deal table stood roughly centre, duly attended by a three-legged stool on either side; an ancient rocking-chair crouched by the fire, and against the opposite wall was a truly magnificent oak dresser, on which was an array of pewter cups, willow-pattern plates and a gigantic silver meat dish. Large tallow candles, embedded in their own grease on little earthenware saucers, stood on the dresser and on a wide stone ledge which served as a mantelpiece.

A wall had been built at each end of the cave. The one through which they had entered was broken by a normal six by three door, while that at the far end supported what appeared to be a castle gate. It could well have been one of a former pair, possibly the relic of a Royalist castle, and indeed the stone bricks that formed the walls may have been part of the same structure. Great, rust-corroded studs dotted its surface, and on the right-hand side, just under an iron ring, was one of the largest keys James had ever seen.

He went over to the bed, which was situated just beyond the fireplace, and gently patted Lydia's pale face.

'Eat.' The old woman had locked the front door, dropped the key into the folds of her gown, and was now examining the contents of the cooking pot. 'Soon wake.'

Lydia stirred, opened her eyes. For a moment she stared up at James, clearly not understanding what had happened, then she gave a little cry and sat up.

'It's all right, dear,' James spoke softly, 'we're safe. This is the old lady's—cottage.'

'James, I'm cold.'

'You'll soon be warm.' He removed his overcoat and covered her. 'The old thing has something cooking.'

Lydia looked round at the bizarre surroundings and shuddered: 'What is it?'

'A sort of converted cave. Rather sensible when you think; no roof to leak, free from draughts. No doubt this is the way our remote forebears lived.'

'It's weird and it stinks,' she wrinkled her nose, 'how long must we stay?'

'Only until morning, then we'll make our way back to the road and pick up a lift. After you've had something to eat, try to sleep.'

'You won't sleep, will you?' She was like a child, with a child's unreasoning selfishness. 'You'll watch and see that old woman doesn't do—anything?'

'I'll watch.'

She closed her eyes, and he turned his attention to the old woman who was stirring whatever seethed in the pot with a wooden spoon.

'You live here long time?' he found himself slipping into the old woman's telegram mode of speech, so started again. 'You have lived here a long time I should imagine?'

She nodded and took an experimental sip from the wooden spoon.

'Long time.'

'How long?'

She let the residue of liquid in the spoon dribble back into the pot.

'Ice go. I come.'

James fowned: 'You mean, you were born at the end of a particularly bad winter?'

She waved the wooden spoon in an all-embracing gesture.

'All ice. Cornwall no ice. I come.'

He was silent for some minutes, then: 'You mean—you were born in the—ice age?'

She did not answer, and Lydia called. 'James, how long will she be? I'm starving.'

'Not long.' He went over to her and perched on the edge of the bed. 'Guess what? She says she was born in the ice age.'

'Really,' Lydia yawned, 'how long ago was that?'

'I don't know. A hundred million years at least. Perhaps more.'

'That's silly. I said she was cracked.'

'Of course it's impossible. But she's certainly something out of the ordinary. She carried you without effort, and she must be very old. Do you realise she's probably a relic of the ice age at that? Suppose her forebears had lived here for millions of years, and eyewitness accounts were passed down from generation to generation, then she is really sharing a racial memory. After all, Cornwall was the only part of the British Isles not covered by ice, and we know a type of man did live here.'

'Too deep for me,' Lydia yawned again.

'I'd give anything to know the truth.' James stared at the old woman. 'I wouldn't mind betting she isn't completely human. There must have been quite a few others like her around not so long ago. Perhaps they lived in caves, deep down in the earth. Maybe that door leads to a system of tunnels.'

'There you go again.' A frown creased Lydia's forehead. 'Act your age. She's just an old weirdie who lives alone. You'll find them all over the place. Nutty as a fruit cake, and stinking to high heaven.'

The object of their discussion came hobbling over to the bed, bearing a steaming plate of savoury smelling mixture. This she presented to Lydia with the brief instruction: 'Eat.'

Lydia eagerly seized the silver spoon that lay half submerged in the liquid, and took an experimental sip.

'Not bad, a bit pungent if that is the right word, but quite good.'

The old woman now turned her attention to James. 'Eat.'

He sat down on one of the three-legged stools and took up a spoon, while pretending not to notice their strange hostess, who soon discarded her spoon and drank direct from the plate, then clawed chunks of meat into her mouth.

'Your plates and spoons,' he found himself speaking loudly, as though to a deaf person, 'they are very old?'

'Ugh,' the old woman was using her shawl as a serviette, 'house—war.'

'You mean a house was bombed during the last war, and you . . . ?'

He stopped, it seemed impolite to suggest she might have indulged in an orgy of looting, but the old woman was shaking her head.

'Long-hair, short-hair war.'

'Good God!' James called across to Lydia, 'she's talking about the Civil War. Roundheads and Cavaliers.'

'Nonsense,' Lydia was scraping her plate vigorously. 'I enjoyed that. Anything else?'

'I shouldn't think so.' He nodded amiably to the old woman. 'That was very nice. We are grateful.'

She got up, trotted over to the dresser and returned with a stone bottle and two pewter cups. Into each one she poured a generous measure of amber-coloured liquid.

'Drink. Good. Sleep.'

'Doesn't waste words, does she?' Lydia remarked.

'Hush, she'll hear you.'

'She's deaf, darling,' Lydia was sitting up on the bed,

tightly wrapped in her fur coat, now the very picture of good humour, 'and nutty to boot.' She made a face. 'Me Tarzan, you Jane.'

It did seem that the old woman either did not hear, or did not understand what was said, for she carried a full cup over to Lydia and repeated her brief instruction: 'Drink.'

James drank from his cup. The contents tasted like old peach brandy; a beautiful smooth liqueur that glided down his throat and exploded a delicious warm bomb in his stomach.

'Careful,' he warned, 'it's got a kick like a mule.'

'Who cares?' Lydia emptied her cup, 'we're not going anywhere.'

'True.' James found a little of his natural caution slipping away. 'It's certainly good stuff.' He now addressed the old woman with the tone of voice, and vocabulary, one uses to a dim-witted foreigner: 'Very good. Old, yes?' He patted his cup. 'This very old? You keep long time?'

The old woman nodded.

'Grandfather, grandfather old.'

'Yours or mine?' He drained his cup and did not object when it was refilled. 'If they drank this in the ice age, it sure must have kept out the cold.' Suddenly he was finding difficulty in expressing himself. 'Your grandfather, or mine, or somebody—they make from peaches—yes?'

'No,' said the old woman.

'No.' James realised his head was wagging from side to side, and there was nothing he could do about it. 'Then how make you . . . From what make you . . . ?'

'Blood,' said the old woman.

James repeated 'Blood,' before unconsciousness closed in, and for a time he was lost in a place of utter darkness.

Sight was the first sense that came back to life; the fire had been made up, a fresh log was blazing and blue smoke was clawing at the chimney opening. Then hearing returned; the log was spluttering, a series of angry spits, and the old woman was crooning a tuneless dirge while she undressed Lydia.

James was half-reclining in the rocking-chair, his legs stretched out before him, and his brain, which seemed reluctant to resume its duties, noted without either alarm or particular interest that his limbs were powerless. He could not move, speak, or even blink.

Lydia had a beautiful body, that was a fact he had always accepted. When the old woman slung that naked body over her shoulder and transported it to the now cleared table, the artist could only admire the clean contours of her back, and how her long hair tumbled down in a mass of amber glory. If only the old hag would stand still.

But the old woman did not stand still. She slumped Lydia down upon the table, trotted over to the dresser, and returned with a pile of stout cord. The crooning was now high-pitched, and the tiny feet were dancing, or rather marking time, while she doubled Lydia's legs, bound calf to thigh, then bent her arms at the elbows and secured them firmly.

'She looks like a trussed chicken,' a silent giggle ran across his brain, 'ready for the oven.'

The old woman stepped back and seemed very satisfied with her work, for she chuckled, then hugged herself, and did a little dance of pure joy.

'Good . . . good . . .'

'What about the stuffing?' James wanted to point out that Lydia was not ready for eating, and felt unreasonably annoyed when his body refused to pass on this information.

The old woman, still in a state of great excitement, ran to the big door, the one James was certain had been a castle gate, and eagerly turned the immense key. She grabbed the iron ring, and pulled. With a rust-corroded scream, the door slid open. A blast of cold air made the candle flames tremble and caused Lydia's hair to writhe like Medusa's snakes. From beyond the door came the chatter of running water, and a harsh sound, such as a pair of bellows might make when the valves are leaking.

The old woman shuffled forward a few paces, then called out: 'Dunmore! Dunmore!'

A scraping sound. Then a mighty phlegm-choked cough—a hawking, disgusting spitting—a series of explosive cracks, followed by a deep groan.

'Eat,' said the old woman.

The rasping—was it breathing?—became louder, then faster; a steady crunch-crunch, suggesting the approach of heavy footsteps, and again there was a groaning cough and a throat-clearing spit.

'Eat,' repeated the old woman, then backed rapidly into the room.

It came into view—into James's view, and filled the doorway, and at once his brain was blasted into full, terror-stricken awareness.

It was a man formed some twenty feet high, perhaps seven feet across the shoulders, with an enormous melon-shaped head and a pair of saucer-sized eyes that were all black pupils. He was covered by thick, grey hair, save for an area around the eyes. The tufts that sprouted from the ears and nostrils were reddish in colour, and stiff, like pig's bristle. But one thing was certain, the—giant—was old and sick. A yellow, blood-flecked fluid was dribbling down from the flaring nostrils, and the hair-covered skin hung in great folds about the mighty frame. The old woman pointed to the trussed figure of Lydia, who was just returning to consciousness and emitting small whimpering sounds.

'Eat. Good.'

There was sheer, stark terror, and a great pain in his head, and a mighty voice shouting at him to get his drugged body back into action and save Lydia. Save Lydia! But it was her fault—her selfishness was to blame. They should be in the car, on their way to Lizard, and that—that—thing . . . It was monstrous, at the same time it was beautiful. It had the beauty of sheer ugliness, and his fingers twitched in their desire for a paintbrush—charcoal . . . But he must save Lydia. That first . . . afterwards . . . afterwards . . . His arms and legs began to move, his brain seemed to expand, become a seething mass of boiling hate, only he was not sure at what, or whom, the hate was directed. Then something snapped, the pain was gone. He rose to his feet, strong, fearless . . .

The giant lumbered forward and reached down one hair-covered, thumbless hand. A finger coiled round a cord, and tugged; the cord snapped, and Lydia screamed, a terrible, ear-torturing shriek.

The strange new James bent down (how coolly his brain was working) and ripped up a length of the grease-coated, half-rotted matting. He tossed one end on to the fire. It instantly flared up into an orange flame. Swinging the blazing matting round his head, James advanced towards the giant, who backed away, clearly more surprised than frightened, while the old woman danced a little reel of fear.

'No . . . no. He last one. No more. All dead. No hurt. Dunmore last.'

She rushed at James, who seized her shawl and pushed. She was flung to the floor, leaving the shawl in his hand, and he had a brief glimpse of a bald, crater-pitted head . . . then he flung the blazing matting round one tree-sized leg.

The thick hair took fire, and a cascade of tiny flames spluttered upwards, accompanied by a mist of blue, evil-smelling smoke. The monster's roar rose to a shrill scream, and it spun round and started to hop wildly across the cave, vainly trying to rub the flames out with its hands. This only made matters worse, for now the arm hair was frizzling, and the flames leapt to the matted growth on its chest, rushing with amazing speed towards the beard. All the while a little bald-headed figure ran round the blazing colossus, flapping uselessly with a blanket, mingling her shrieks with his, dancing, weaving, like a tiny, mangy dog. The beard went up in one orange flame, the long head hair was for a moment a splendid, blazing torch, then there was just blue smoke, blackened flesh, and several tons of pain-racked rage.

The old woman howled like a dog, then sank to the floor, and James stared with unblinking eyes at her head. The skull was round, and pitted in places, as though the bone had disintegrated, and in these craters, like sun-starved weeds, grew little tufts of white hair. Due possibly to blood pressure, these minute growths throbbed up and down, as though caressed by some silent wind.

James walked calmly towards the table, and after fumbling for his pocket knife, cut the cords which still bound Lydia. She was sobbing, and trembling violently; he pulled her from the table and nodded in the direction of the bed.

'Get dressed,' he said curtly.

'James . . . I can't walk.'

'Don't be silly. Get dressed.'

Dunmore was moaning, a hideous, groaning whine, and every now and again the old woman raised her head and howled up at him. Perhaps she touched one burnt leg, or maybe the giant in a frenzy of pain-inspired rage struck at the nearest living creature; whatever the reason, one great foot suddenly rose, then came crashing down. The old woman disintegrated into a mass of crushed bone and flattened flesh, and Lydia screamed.

'James, oh my God, James. Get me out of here.'

James smiled, a strange, mirthless grimace, and he spoke coldly.

'Shut up, you silly cow.'

Dunmore looked down at all that remained of the old woman with an almost comical expression of concern. He prodded the flattened mess with one huge misshapen toe; the head rolled free and came bouncing across the room like an overgrown black billiard ball. James picked it up. Within the small craters the tufts of white hair still moved gently. Sighing deeply, he tossed it carelessly aside.

The giant began to cough, great gurgling roars, then blood poured out of his mouth and nose; a scarlet stream that gushed down his black chest, splashed into a rapidly spreading pool between the splayed feet. His descent was slow, like an oak tree that has resisted the storms of centuries and is now brought low by the axe of a pygmy. He slithered down the wall, his legs sliding across the floor until he came to rest in a sitting position, his great eyes wide open, seemingly glazed with astonishment. The blood ceased to flow, and he was still.

'Is he—dead?' asked Lydia, then started to giggle.

'Dead,' James nodded, 'dead.'

He walked slowly over to the bed and picked up his overcoat; from one pocket he produced an artist's sketch-book, then moved back to the table. He then took up a three-legged stool, which he placed between Dunmore's widespread feet. He sat down and opened the sketch-book, then, after a moment's contemplation, took out a pencil and began to draw.

Presently, the girl touched his shoulder, but with an impatient gesture he shrugged her hand away. She ran to the front door and tugged at the handle; the door was locked. The wood was age-toughened oak, and the key—it must be in that mass of splintered bones and mangled flesh.

She tore back to the seated figure and hammered clenched fists on to unresponsive shoulders. 'James, we must get out. Please, please listen.'

He raised a blank, white face; the eyes were as cold as moorland snow.

'Don't you understand, woman? That . . .' he pointed his pencil at the blood-drenched corpse, 'that was the very last one. The very last Cornish giant. She said so. And if I hadn't interfered, you might have saved him. White meat was all he wanted. Soft, warm, white meat.'

With clenched fist stuffed into mouth, Lydia backed away, then giggling softly she moved slowly towards that little pile of crushed bone, wrapped in a crumpled, blood-soaked gown. She probed with trembling fingers. Gingerly at first, fastidiously, then, as panic grew to madness, wildly, she tore the cloth, clawing at the pulped mess, until she gave a loud cry of triumph and snatched at a piece of rough metal. The key was quite large, but it was rust-corroded, and the important part—that which turned the lock—was broken. Lydia stared at the useless key for a long time, then she retreated to the bed and sat there, moaning softly. Gradually, as the fire died and an icy coldness seeped into the cave, the full horror became apparent to her. She was locked up for ever with a madman.

James continued to work, unmoved, his pencil racing across the paper. After all, there was not much time. Soon the candles would burn out, and there would be darkness. Eternal darkness.